JEAN SAUNDERS
Partners in Love

Published by Silhouette Books New York
America's Publisher of Contemporary Romance

Silhouette Books by Jean Saunders

The Kissing Time (ROM #153)
Love's Sweet Magic (ROM #216)
The Language of Love (ROM #243)
Taste the Wine (ROM #261)
Partners in Love (ROM #289)

SILHOUETTE BOOKS, a Division of Simon & Schuster, Inc.
1230 Avenue of the Americas, New York, N.Y. 10020

Distributed by Pocket Books

ISBN: 0-671-57289-X

First Silhouette Books printing April, 1984

10 9 8 7 6 5 4 3 2 1

Map by Ray Lundgren

America's Publisher of Contemporary Romance

Printed in the U.S.A.

"Try to Deny That We're The Same Kind of People, You and I. . . ."

Luke spoke roughly against her bruised lips. "We meet on equal terms, with the same needs, the same desires, and your responses tell me you want me as much as I want you—"

Robin pushed him away from her, sitting as far from him as she could in the car, her green eyes blazing.

"You're like all men," she lashed out at him. "You think all you have to do is turn on the charm and women will grovel at your feet—"

"That wasn't quite what I had in mind." Luke grinned. "But maybe it wouldn't have worked after all. I'm not sure I could cope with a secretary with the looks of an angel and the temper of the devil."

JEAN SAUNDERS
describes herself as a compulsive writer and has written more than 23 novels and over 600 short stories. A participating member of several British writers' organizations, including the Romantic Novelists Association, Jean enjoys anything to do with writing and writers.

Dear Reader:

I'd like to take this opportunity to thank you for all your support and encouragement of Silhouette Romances.

Many of you write in regularly, telling us what you like best about Silhouette, which authors are your favorites. This is a tremendous help to us as we strive to publish the best contemporary romances possible.

All the romances from Silhouette Books are for you, so enjoy this book and the many stories to come.

Karen Solem
Editor-in-Chief
Silhouette Books

Partners in Love

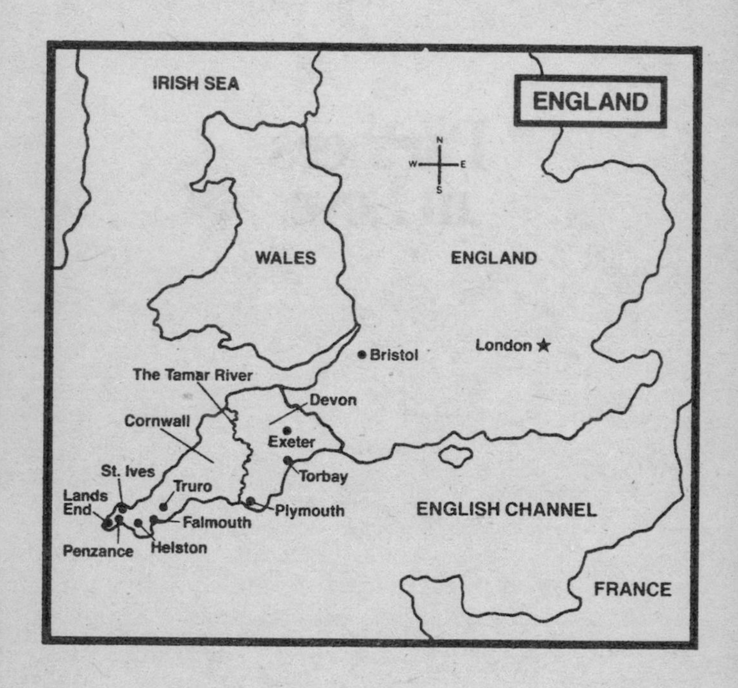
ENGLAND
IRISH SEA
N
W
E
S
WALES
ENGLAND
Bristol
London
The Tamar River
Devon
Cornwall
Exeter
Torbay
St. Ives
Truro
Lands End
Plymouth
Falmouth
Penzance
Helston
ENGLISH CHANNEL
FRANCE

Chapter One

The blissful peace of the mellow autumn afternoon was suddenly shattered. Robin lay where she was on the fine, warm sand of the cove, her eyes determinedly closed. She didn't exactly own the beach, she reminded herself, but she had always felt it to be her special place, one that the tourists seldom found because of its seclusion on the sheer-sided Cornish coast.

The sound of muted male voices was an intrusion. She needed this solitude, and realising that the voices had momentarily paused, as if in surprise at finding anyone in the cove, she dug her pink fingernails into the soft sand by her sides. The very last thing she wanted right now was for some cheerful daytripper to wander into her preserves and try to chat her up.

Robin was perfectly aware that she would be a target for a particular type of male tourist. With her delicate heart-shaped face and her unexpectedly green eyes, combined with silken corn-coloured hair and the honeyed tan she acquired each year from her native Cornish sun, Robin was used to male attention.

There had been a time when she might have gathered up all her beach gear and made her way back up the steep hillside as she became aware that the voices were coming nearer. But why should she leave?

Her green eyes remained tightly closed behind her huge sunglasses until she sensed a shadow falling across her body. Only then did she open them a fraction and see the large dark shape of a man standing beside her. Because the sun was behind him, Robin couldn't discern his features, but even from her supine position she could see that he was tall. At that moment he almost blotted out the sun completely; almost . . . except for the odd little effect of the sunlight glinting around his head, dazzling Robin's eyes in the way of the diamond-ring phenomenon.

"You're standing in my space," she said abruptly.

"I apologise." His voice was slightly mocking. His accent wasn't local, Robin detected at once; neither was it unpleasing or particularly foreign—*foreign* being the way a true daughter of Cornwall referred to the "grockles," the folk from up-country England.

"I wasn't aware you'd taken a lease on this particular patch of sand," the man went on, "though you fill it to perfection, if I may say so."

Robin would rather he didn't say so. As he still hadn't moved away, she glared up at him, her temper, never slow to rise, beginning to make itself apparent. As if something of her mood got across to him, the stranger stepped slightly to one side, and the full heat of the afternoon sun warmed Robin's body once more.

Then she could see the man properly. To her surprise he didn't look like the average tourist. For one thing, he wasn't dressed casually enough: He wore a dark high-neck sweater, a tweed sports jacket and dark trousers. His face was craggy rather than good-looking, with keen eyes and a sardonic twist to the mouth. Because of her sunglasses, Robin couldn't determine their colour.

She didn't care what colour they were, anyway, she thought angrily. The realisation that the man was allowing his gaze to wander lazily over her body was enough to make her sit up immediately.

"Do you always stare like that at strangers?" she was nettled enough to say.

"If they look as good as you, why not?" he shot back, his eyes lingering over the firmness of her breasts in the yellow bikini top and following the dipping curve of her waist and the feminine roundness of her hips to her long, shapely legs and small feet. It was a look that made Robin squirm, and it wasn't only the heat of the sun that sent the blood coursing through her veins.

He had a hell of a nerve, she thought furiously. She threw on her white mesh beach top with an angry gesture.

"Excuse me, I was about to leave," she said pointedly. "The cove loses its charm when it's invaded—"

To Robin's surprise he bent down and put a restraining hand on her arm. She could feel the strength in his fingers, warm on her skin through the cotton mesh.

"Please don't go because of me. I'm sorry if I've interrupted your sunbathing. I hadn't expected to find someone like you here, and you rather took me by surprise, that's all. Just pretend I'm not here."

His words were odd enough to intrigue her. And Robin knew she couldn't ignore him if he intended to stay. It was far better that she went back home. The evening ahead of her promised to be a disagreeable one as far as she was concerned, and for her father's sake it was best that she didn't work herself into a worse mood.

"I was going anyway," she said coolly, jerking her arm out of the man's grasp.

"That's a pity," he replied, looking into her eyes. Robin removed her sunglasses and her heart gave a little jolt. The stranger's eyes were unusually blue and his nose very straight, and there were deep indentations at the sides of his strong mouth. He was a man who knew what he liked and usually got it, Robin guessed, though why it should interest her in the slightest, she couldn't imagine.

She looked around her with a strange feeling of desperation. The cove was so secluded that she never gave a thought to possible danger when she went down there alone. She had been going there all her life; it was her place . . . but surely if she had heard male voices earlier, there should be more than one man around. Unless she had been having hallucinations.

Then away to the right of her she saw another man with his back to the soft, slow, glassy swell of the tide, gazing towards the hillside through binoculars. Robin felt anger replace her feeling of alarm. Were they snoopers or just voyeurs? How long had she been in their sights through the binoculars before they made their way down the steps on the hillside? She felt suddenly exposed, as if, unknown to her, the two of them had been observing her for hours. By now the man standing with insolent ease at her side might know every curve and line of her body as intimately as a lover, and Robin felt a surge of colour stain her cheeks at the thought. She stood up, shaking the sand from her hair with an angry swing of her head, not missing the way the man's eyes strayed to the glorious mane of golden hair.

"I don't know what you're doing here, but I think I

prefer the honest-to-goodness beach wolf to someone who creeps up on me when I'm enjoying the peace and quiet," Robin snapped.

Now that she was standing up, she realised the man was a good head and shoulders taller than she was. She slipped her feet into her beach shoes, wishing she had high heels on so that she didn't feel at such a psychological disadvantage. She raised her chin and glared angrily into the man's eyes.

To her sudden fury, the glint of a smile appeared around the man's mouth, and the somewhat ruthless hardness of his face softened a little. Around the blue eyes Robin saw the crease of laughter lines, but she was in no mood to be patronised. All she saw was the condescension of the superior male.

"If it's a beach wolf you want, I'm sure I'd be more than willing to oblige. . . ."

"I don't want anything, except to be left alone."

Robin snatched up her canvas beach bag and started to walk away. A soft breeze from the sea blew a salt tang into her nostrils, mingled with the unmistakable scent of pine, which Robin realised came from the man himself. He leaned towards her, the smile vanishing from his face as quickly as it came.

"I'm sure you'll have no trouble getting your wish," he said frostily. "If this is an example of Cornish hospitality, I'm almost sorry I came."

"So am I!" Robin tossed back as she made her way to the foot of the rough steps. "You're obviously not cut out for the ways of simple folk like us!"

She felt his eyes on her retreating figure as she climbed the wide grass steps more swiftly than usual. By the time she reached the top she had a pain in her side and her breathing was more rapid than usual. At this rate she'd have a heart attack like Mrs. Fowler. Robin swallowed, remembering briefly the shock of discovering her charming employer had died in her sleep six weeks earlier, leaving Robin feeling as bereft as if she'd lost a close relative—and sending her limping back to Cornwall, metaphorically speaking, the way an injured animal seeks refuge in places dear and familiar. . . .

She paused for breath on the headland where the wild moorland grasses and bracken sighed in the warm breeze. The whisper of bracken and the scent of yarrow and clover had always had a relaxing effect on her, but this afternoon she barely noticed them.

Robin was appalled at herself for the way she had reacted to a complete stranger. Her father had always said she should curb her fiery temper, and at twenty-three she thought she had managed to do so. But the man had riled her, and she had reacted with typical rashness.

From her high vantage point above the silvery-grey shimmer of the sea and the golden sand of the cove, Robin could see the two men standing close together now. Of the stranger's companion she had seen little, except that he was a mite younger and less interesting a personality.

She was shocked even to consider that the man had a personality worth noting—but, undeniably he did. In fact, if she had met him under different circumstances, Robin knew she would have found him more than intriguing. He was the kind of man whom women did notice. There was a raw sensuality about him that reached out to a woman. Robin gave an involuntary shiver as the object of her thoughts suddenly lifted his head and seemed to look directly into her eyes.

From that distance it was impossible to see his expression, but remembering how he had looked at her in the cove, Robin felt her heartbeat quicken. The man lifted his hand as if in mock salute and she turned away furiously, angry with herself for letting him see that she had been watching him. A man of his arrogance would never believe she had been doing anything else, Robin thought with disgust, even more annoyed with herself for acknowledging he would be right.

She made her way across the wide stretch of moorland with the sun still beating down with pleasant heat on her back and shoulders. Autumn came late in Cornwall, and it often seemed as if summer were reluctant to go. This particular sheltered part of the Helford River valley, where the river met the sea, was blessed, Robin thought. It had warm winds and soft, mellow days with none of the Atlantic gales that ravaged some of the more exposed coasts, except on rare occasions.

It was all so beautifully unspoiled, she thought, with a small sigh of pleasure. At least, it always had been, and Robin had thought it would continue to be so. But two weeks before, when she had finally come back home, she had found her father in an unusually keyed-up frame of mind. Naturally glad to see his daughter home, he nevertheless treated her a little warily, the way he used to when she was a rather rebellious teen-ager and he'd said that dealing with her moods was like treading over broken glass. Exasperated after several days of hedging about, Robin demanded to know what was wrong.

He had looked at her uneasily.

"Come on, Dad, I know you well enough to know when you've got something on your mind. If you're worried about my being out of a job and still pining over Mrs. Fowler, you needn't be. I'll find something else. . . ."

"You know I'd never worry about that, Robin. You know you're welcome to stay here and look after me in my old age, but I can't imagine the soft life being enough for you."

"You're not old, and stop trying to soft-soap me,"

she said affectionately. "But you can't fool me, either, so let's have it."

James Pollard had smiled faintly.

"I see that caring for Mrs. Fowler did nothing to stem your impatience, and I might have known you'd soon wheedle it out of me. . . ."

"You aren't ill, are you, Dad?" It was something Robin hadn't considered. She looked at him swiftly, but he looked the same as ever, a robust grey-haired man in his middle fifties, for whom early retirement from a businessman's life seven years earlier upon inheriting the lovely old manor house in Truro in which he now lived had been a delight to both him and his daughter. No, Robin thought with some relief, he certainly didn't look ill. He shook his head quickly, confirming it.

"All right, then. I can't hide it from you forever anyway," he had said briskly. Robin had tensed, a sixth sense telling her she was about to hear something of importance. But whatever she had expected, it was nothing like the shock she received.

"I've decided to lease some of the land belonging to the estate, Robin. It's little more than wild moor now, and of no use for anything unless someone wanted to build there, and I can't imagine a person wanting a house half buried in the lee of the hillside with all that rough woodland behind it to the north. I'd never even considered selling or leasing any part of the estate, but a property developer got in touch with me and made me an offer too good to refuse. Of course, I never really thought it would come off." James shrugged, avoiding his daughter's horrified eyes, and blundered on. "There was planning permission to obtain—the plans to be approved by me as well as the town and country planners—but this fellow could charm the birds off the trees, I reckon, because it's all gone through."

Robin found her voice at last.

"You don't mean the land above my cove!" she'd spluttered furiously. "Dad, you can't! That's my special place—"

"I know you always used to call it that, darling, but that was when you were a child and used to go down there for holidays with your great-aunt." Knowing just what her reaction would be, James was sharper than he'd intended. "You're too old to indulge in childish fantasies now, Robin. I'm still a businessman at heart, and when a golden opportunity comes my way, I'm still capable of seeing the potential and grasping it. It's not as if I'm selling outright. I'm only leasing the land, so I shall be a kind of partner in the development. In time the interest in it will revert to you."

Robin had been too recently involved with the harrowing details of Mrs. Fowler's bequests to want to linger on any future prospects from her father's business deal. One phrase stuck in her mind as he spoke and she seized on it now.

"What development?" she demanded to know, her green eyes blazing like emeralds in her flushed face. Her father sighed.

"It's to be a tourist development." He confirmed her worst fears. "A series of one-storey self-catering apartments that will be unseen from the surrounding areas so as not to detract from the rural environment."

"Oh, how could you! Whether we see them or not, they'll be there, won't they? Dozens of tourists will be infiltrating every summer and moving in with their rotten ice creams and blaring transistors," she raged.

"You're being very stupid, Robin, and also very selfish," her father had said coldly. "How often will you be here to see any of them? You've said yourself that you'll be looking for a new job soon, and if you enjoy the peace and tranquility of our Cornish beaches, why shouldn't we let other people enjoy them?"

"That's just the point! They won't be peaceful any longer, once you let hordes of tourists in."

"If you'd take the trouble to look at the plans, you'd see there won't be hordes of them. The development is only for six apartments. There simply isn't space for more."

"Thank God!"

"And anyway, it isn't directly above your cove, as you call it. The ground is too steep there. It's along to the right, above the wider bay, where the ground levels out a little. The apartments will be stepped to give maximum privacy—"

"I don't want to hear about it," Robin had snapped. She knew that she was being unreasonable and that her father was probably looking forward to being involved in this project. The role of gentleman land-owner didn't sit altogether comfortably on him, and the fact that he was disappointed in her violent reaction to his news made her feel ashamed but unable to stop herself from lashing out at him verbally.

James could be as stubborn as his daughter. "Very well. But you will at least be civil when Mr. Burgess and his surveyor arrive in a couple of weeks to take some preliminary assessments. I've asked them to dinner, since they'll be staying in Helston overnight. I would have asked them to stay here, but I anticipated some kind of childish flouncing about."

She'd glared at him speechlessly, knowing his words held too much truth in them to be denied. Was it childish to want to cling to one's heritage, to a little bit of Cornwall that was very dear to her? Hot quick tears had sprung to her eyes. Knowing how much her reaction hurt her father, because it was his heritage, too, she had run to his arms, much as she had done when she was a child, and mumbled that she'd try to be polite for his sake, but that she was never going to like the unknown Mr. Burgess for destroying her dreamworld.

Robin's footsteps faltered a little as she walked on that lovely autumn day towards the stone-built manor house that had known several generations of Pollards before her. Solid and with the windows glinting in the sunlight, it was the refuge she'd run to after her employer's sad demise. But now, after several weeks' recuperation, Robin was aware of a growing restlessness within her. Pollard Manor was marvellous to come home to—and her cove would always hold a special place in her heart—but she was no longer a child. Maybe Mrs. Fowler's death had shown her that too. She had had to cope with a lot in the past weeks; there had been no relatives nearer than Australia, and Robin had been left to sort out the estate with the solicitor. But she was a woman now, and she needed to work. Her father was right in one thing: She couldn't stay there idly forever. . . .

Gnawing away at the back of her mind was something else, though—something of more immediate importance. A suspicion was forming in her mind. She didn't want to think about it, but there was no way she could avoid it. Back in the cove she had been too incensed with the stranger's insolent masculinity to question what he was doing there, even though he had looked nothing like the usual tourist. And what about his companion? Robin remembered the way the other man had been scrutinising the hillside. She'd wondered briefly whether he had been bird-watching—either the feathered or the female variety, she thought dryly—but now there was something else she remembered.

The stranger had made an odd comment: "I wasn't aware you'd taken a lease on this particular patch of sand . . ."

It was that use of the word *lease* that did it. Robin felt her heart begin to pound sickeningly. It had to be, of course—the unknown Mr. Burgess, who was coming to dinner that evening and with whom her father was entering into some kind of dubious partnership. Who was going to profit most? Robin wondered cynically. Well, she'd keep a very shrewd eye on things tonight, and if there was any hint of dirty business, she'd clamp down on it fast. Her father knew all about buying and selling in the retail book trade, but she was willing to bet the stranger at the beach would win hands down when it came to big business deals. And Robin wasn't going to let him get the better of her father. . . .

She had the advantage over Mr. Burgess. She had guessed his identity, while she doubted if he even knew she existed. She dressed with care that evening. If he thought he was dealing with simple folk, as she had referred to herself, he could think again. Robin looped her golden hair up into a more sophisticated style and wore long drop earrings that gleamed in the light. She dressed in a simple black cocktail dress with a deep neckline and caressing figure-moulding shape. On her feet she wore slender high-heeled sandals with diamanté straps that would put her a little nearer the stranger's height. Her face glowed with the honeyed suntan and the soft lip gloss and green eyeshadow she'd subtly applied. She knew very well what she was doing and that she looked fantastic. She'd let him think she was playing up to him, and she'd find out just exactly what his game was in developing property down there at the back of nowhere. Instinct told her he wasn't just doing it for the benefit of the tourists. He was in it for himself, and she had every intention of letting him know she despised him for it. He'd have a shock when he saw her and discovered just who she was.

The guests had already arrived by the time Robin made her entrance down the long curving staircase into the drawing room, where she heard her father laughing over some little joke with his two companions. For a moment Robin hesitated. Maybe it wasn't the stranger she'd met that day after all. What a fool she'd feel then, after going to all this trouble. She didn't admit that she'd be more than a little piqued if it wasn't him.

Not for a moment would she allow the thought to enter her mind that she wanted to see the admiration the stranger had already accorded her, acknowledging the unspoken attraction between a man and a woman, sweeter than any words, an exhilaration of the senses. Robin heard the stranger laugh and knew it was he.

She pushed open the drawing-room door and three people turned towards her, different expressions on their faces: her father, slightly anxious, mutely hopeful for her acceptance of the situation and her support; the young man, whom Robin assumed to be the surveyor, and who now seemed struck totally dumb at seeing this golden vision in front of him; and the stranger—the nonstranger, Robin thought—who was now wearing an elegant dark brown velvet dinner jacket and immaculate white shirt, his legs encased in beautifully pressed trousers. The creases at the sides of his blue eyes were more defined now, and there was a triumphant gleam in his eyes as his gaze possessed her for the briefest moment, but long enough to take in every inch of her appearance. Then her father was making the introductions and she learned that his name was Luke Burgess.

Smiling sweetly, Robin held out her hand. The second Luke took it in his own, holding it with seductive gentleness as his forefinger made tingling little movements against her palm, unseen by anyone else, Robin knew that he had known all along who she was.

"It's so good to see you again, Miss Pollard." It was just as if he knew she was dressed up like that for a purpose, she raged, even while she smiled sweetly at him. And he was outplaying her at her own game.

Chapter Two

"Have you two met before?" James Pollard asked at once.

Robin eased her hand out of Luke's. She could still feel the pressure of his fingers and resisted the urge to rub at her palm to rid herself of the tingling sensation his touch had evoked. She turned to her father.

"Just briefly at the cove today." She spoke blandly enough, but her mouth trembled slightly. Normally she said "my cove," but tonight the full force of knowing it was no longer exclusively hers was hitting her between the eyes. It had never been really hers, Robin thought honestly, but that didn't alter the fact that it was this man who was taking away a childhood dream.

"I thought it must be your lovely daughter, Mr. Pollard," Luke said easily. "Anyone taking the trouble to climb down those steep steps in the hillside had to be local, and since this house is the only one around here, I put two and two together."

So he can count, too, Robin thought sarcastically.

"We've always liked it that way," she said coolly. "Being the only house around here, I mean."

Her eyes clashed with Luke's for a moment, and then she turned to the other man, Bill Withers, to ask what he thought of Cornwall, giving him all her attention and hoping Luke felt the snub as sharply as she had meant it.

"It's a very pleasant part of England," Bill began with enthusiasm, only to pause as he heard James Pollard's chuckle.

"Don't call it England in front of the natives, Bill," he said lightly. "Don't you know we consider them all foreigners east of the Tamar?"

"I thought that was a little piece of folklore put about for the tourists," Luke commented. His fingers stroked the stem of his glass with a small caressing motion, and Robin found her eyes being drawn to the movement against her will. Imagining those same hands caressing her skin, her mouth . . . good grief, what had her father put in her glass tonight! she thought abruptly. She wasn't usually so affected by the appearance of a stranger, especially one who was planning to spoil her private heaven.

She put her glass down on a little table and stared serenely at the man who was causing such a churning inside of her.

"Oh, if you stay down here awhile, I think you'll get the idea that Cornwall is primarily for the Cornish, Mr. Burgess."

"Luke, please," he instructed. "But you must agree that without the tourists it's a dying county. All the statistics prove that you need them. The old fishing industry has petered out; the tin mines are worked out and the mines generally derelict except for a few; the china clay industry is not as prosperous as it once was . . ."

"You've done your homework," Robin had to admit, finding her temper begin to rise at his calm dismissal of the things that had made her home county great. "But we still have our heritage, Mr. Burgess—all right, *Luke,*" she added, at the little quirk of his eyebrows. "We're still a fiercely proud people who don't take kindly to strangers and especially those who come storming down here and expect to change us—"

"Like property developers and tourists," he finished for her.

In the silence that followed, Robin realised that the brief exchange had got a little heated, their voices rising. There was nothing of the genteel visitor about the man, she raged. He was ruthless and dynamic and knew exactly what he wanted. There was a sudden dark gleam in the blue eyes holding hers, and Robin knew with an instant unbidden thrill that he wanted *her.*

It was raw, sensual need that she glimpsed in his eyes for that moment before he veiled the briefly revealed animal desire. But Robin had seen it and recognised it and knew, to her fury, that it had struck an answering spark in her that she despised. Of all the men in the world, she wouldn't let herself fall for this arrogant, macho stranger. . . .

Her father was laughing as Mrs. Drew, the housekeeper-cum-factotum, announced that dinner was ready in the dining room. "You've met your match with Luke, Robin," he said. He was openly amused at finding a man willing to stand up and spar verbally with his headstrong daughter and not flinch after the first few caustic remarks. He'd told her once that she was never going to find a man until she curbed her sharp tongue, and that it would take a strong-willed man to tame her.

Infuriated, Robin remembered his teasing words as

Luke Burgess took her arm to accompany her into the dining room. Again she was aware of the pressure of his touch—of everything about him. And the thought that suddenly stunned her was that here was a man who was man enough to satisfy any woman.

All through dinner she became increasingly aware of the fact that her father and Bill Withers seemed to be holding one conversation, while she and Luke were managing quite well to hold another—one that, to Robin's chagrin, was charged with double meanings. Only now did she realize that Luke Burgess stimulated her mind in a way no man had for a long time. She wasn't yet ready to admit that he stimulated her in other ways, too, and that her feminine response to his masculinity was as inevitable as the changing seasons.

"I take it, Robin, that you know all about our project from your father." He made no pretense at formality, cutting through the social barrier of polite small talk.

Across the candlelit table she managed to glare into his eyes while keeping a reasonable smile on her lips.

"Oh, yes," she cooed. "I haven't paid that much attention to it though. This is not the first time we've had people from the big cities coming down here, thinking they can change us. They've usually gone away again and nothing has come of it."

His blue eyes challenged hers.

"What did you do to them, Robin? Frighten them away with tales of the little people on the misty moors? I'm not so easily put off when I see something I want."

"Really?" Her heart gave a little lurch.

"Besides, my big city, as you call it, isn't so far removed from Cornwall. We're still 'west-country' in Bristol."

So that was why his accent wasn't unfamiliar, Robin realised.

"I'm sure you'd find it terribly boring in the wilds, though, after city life."

"On the contrary, I've seen nothing to bore me yet. In fact, I've been fascinated by all I've seen so far. I intend to get to know it all much more intimately. I believe in giving every new project the vigour it deserves."

He was impossible, Robin fumed. All the while he had been talking, his eyes had left her flushed cheeks and soft mouth and taken their fill of the smooth line of her throat to where the low neckline of her black dress revealed the golden swell of her breasts. Robin watched as he ran the tip of his tongue very lightly over his top lip in a blatant gesture of desire.

He was outrageous! But over and beyond the fury she felt was a new and exalted sensation as the woman in her reacted. He wanted her . . . and although it was too soon—too soon and too unthinkable, because he was the enemy who was infiltrating her domain—the fire of a matching desire was running through her veins like quicksilver.

"Have you met my father before?" She needed to bring the talk back to safer matters and drag her thoughts away from the turbulent emotions inside her.

"We've had several telephone conversations and exchanged letters," Luke replied, taking her cue, as if he knew exactly what he was doing to her and understood when to play it cool, leaving her stranded in confusion. She was unused to the feeling and angered by it.

"Bill and I are staying at a hotel in Helston until tomorrow afternoon. Perhaps you and your father would like to come over during the morning and we can show you our proposals and the architectural plans we've drawn up. I'd like you to be our guests for lunch, and then perhaps we can come back to the site and explain more graphically just how little we intend to change the natural beauty of your particular space."

Luke had deliberately used her own phrase, Robin noticed at once. But he had included her father and Bill Withers in the invitation, and James agreed at once to the idea. It was best that they knew exactly what was going on, Robin decided. They had a stake in all this, and if they had any objections to the plans, there was no reason why they shouldn't speak up and say as much. She had every intention of doing so.

She was beginning to feel like her father's champion. James Pollard wasn't a man to be dazzled by the thought of the money to be gained from the project. He was financially secure, but Robin guessed it was the idea of being involved in a project once more after the years of retirement that intrigued him—and possibly blinded him to the true intentions of these strangers. Robin suddenly saw her new role as protector of her father's interests as the most important one she had ever undertaken, one that hadn't devolved on her before she met Luke Burgess.

Was that only that afternoon, she thought with a little shock? They had progressed so far in such a little time, but it happened like that with some people—people whose lives were destined to be intertwined whether through love or hate or friendship.

"I'm sure a lady of leisure can find something to object to," Luke was saying now. "How do you fill your time, Robin? I can see that your summers consist of lazy days at the beach, and you certainly have the suntan to prove it."

She was quite sure that if her father and Bill hadn't been listening, Luke would have asked her if the tan was over her entire body. The question was there in his eyes. Before she could think of a reply, Luke gave a short laugh.

"And I suppose in the winter you're one of these precious do-gooders who throw themselves into social activities for the community, as daughter of the country squire and all that. Are you?"

He said it teasingly enough for it not to be insulting, and James seemed to think it funny enough. Robin bristled at once, taking the bait.

"Sorry to disappoint you, Luke," she said lightly, not betraying the resentment she felt at his assumption. "I've never been a social butterfly or a do-gooder. In fact, until six weeks ago I was secretary-companion to Elaine Fowler, the pianist. You probably haven't heard of her." She conveyed the impression that he'd be too much of a vulgarian to appreciate good music.

"Didn't she die suddenly at her home in London?" he asked, to her surprise. Robin's throat was momentarily constricted by grief, and she had to swallow back the sharp recollection of that awful morning when she had gone in to awaken her beloved employer. She nodded, acknowledging that at least Luke must read the newspapers.

"That's right. So, far from spending the summer lazing about on beaches," she added cuttingly, "I've spent my time coping with a lady who drove herself too hard, considering her years, but died the way she would have wanted: loved by her public."

She blinked the unexpected mist of tears from her eyes, not wanting to fall apart at the dinner table and furious with Luke Burgess for stirring up so many memories of a sweet woman who had given pleasure to millions throughout her career.

"And what about you?" She put a caustic note into her voice. "What do you do all day? Sit behind a big desk, sticking little pins into a map deciding which part of the country to disrupt next?"

This time it was Bill Withers who couldn't resist a

laugh. Robin glanced at him, seeing his round face alight with admiration for his companion. Obviously Bill was a fan of Luke's.

"I'd better put you right there, Robin. Luke is a terrific architect in his own right, though he works closely with the top man in the firm, Roy Hutchings. I reckon Luke could cope with this project blindfolded, though; and far from sitting behind a desk all day, he keeps his finger firmly on the pulse of everything that goes on and is hardly ever in the office when anybody wants him. He can be a hard taskmaster, but any client who goes to Burgess Developments knows he's getting a first-class job done."

"Thanks for the plug," Luke said dryly.

"Well, there's nothing like getting so spontaneous a recommendation from one of your own colleagues," James said warmly, clearly impressed. "Now, if we've all finished, perhaps we can go into the drawing room for coffee and liqueurs."

Robin went ahead of the men. Luke's impression of her had been totally wrong, but her ideas about him had also been wrong. She had thought him a figure-head, no more . . . though she should have known better. A man as aggressive and hard as Luke Burgess would obviously not be content to sit behind a desk all day. He was ambitious, too; she had sensed that from the beginning. Her earlier suspicions that her father was being coerced into leasing his land still lingered. She wouldn't embarrass her father that evening by mentioning them.

Bill was becoming more voluble as the four of them relaxed in the drawing room and the aroma of freshly ground coffee filled the air. Robin bit into a crisp after-dinner mint chocolate and hid a smile as the young surveyor elaborated on his boss's character, as if he'd taken on the defender's role himself.

Luke sat opposite her, and although she listened attentively to Bill, she kept Burgess in the periphery of her vision and knew just how often his eyes were upon her. It was almost as if there were really only the two of them in that softly lit room and the conversation around them was merely filling the time until they could be together.

She must be going crazy, Robin thought angrily. For a moment she let her gaze move away from Bill as he talked animatedly to her father, then met Luke's blue eyes, which held hers captive as surely as if he had put his arms around her. She was almost mesmerised by the force of his personality and the certainty that he intended to prove it was stronger than hers. The dominant male asserting himself. There were somc things she knew about him by an instinct as old as time, Robin thought tremulously, a strange and unfamiliar weakness enveloping her as she felt herself drawn to the intensity of his gaze.

She knew that here was a man who was capable of great tenderness as well as brute strength; who would love a woman in any way she desired to be loved, wantonly or gently; who would know how to seduce with the slightest touch or a nuance of his voice. Robin dragged her eyes away from him, hearing Bill address her.

"Luke has his own hero, Robin. You have heard of the great Victorian engineer Isambard Kingdom Brunel, of course? It was he who built the railway bridge over the river Tamar, linking Devon and Cornwall, and brought the Great Western Railway all the way from London to the far west."

"'God's Wonderful Railway.'" Robin nodded, giving the affectionate nickname for the line.

"That's right." Bill grinned. "We all reckon Luke was born a hundred years too late. He should have been scrambling about with that fanatic Brunel, bridge-building and tunnel-digging, and then turning his talents to the railway and ships. . . ."

"Give it a rest, Bill." Luke grinned back. "I'm not a one-man industry. It takes a team of people to complete a project. Even Brunel knew that."

"He had the ideas, though, and that's where the two of you are alike. The ideas and the enthusiasm—"

It was getting to be a mutual admiration society, Robin thought. But Bill was revealing another facet of Luke's character that she hadn't known about. She didn't know him. And after tomorrow it was unlikely they would meet again, except on rare occasions. Even if he came down to Cornwall to keep an eye on the work, which she didn't doubt he would do, she must start looking around for a new job. It wasn't in her nature to be idle, despite Luke's first impression of her, and he was annoyingly right about one thing: In that part of the country, there was little possibility of her getting the kind of secretarial work she would prefer—something more interesting than a bland office routine, because after the excitement of working for Elaine Fowler, it was going to be difficult to accept anything less.

The thought that Luke Burgess would be going out of her life so soon after storming into it sent a pang of regret running through her. But Robin wasn't the type of woman who could sit around, patiently waiting for the next time he would appear on site; neither could she waste her life mooning over a man who must have had his share of women. He might even be married. That sudden realisation was enough to set her pulse racing. She spoke before she could stop herself.

"How does your wife cope with your being away on site a lot, Bill?" It was to him she spoke first, turning as if with an afterthought to Luke. "And yours—or aren't you married?"

"Not yet," Luke said, his words meaning anything or nothing. Then he relented. "Bill is engaged to a lovely girl, but I haven't found anyone I'd ask to share my life—unless you're applying for the job, Robin. You're free at the moment, aren't you?"

"I'm not that desperate," she snapped.

She saw his grin and knew he'd seen right through the questioning, damn him.

"You're getting into the lingo though," he observed. "Referring to the building area as 'on site' tells me you're getting more interested than you were at first."

Robin forgot all about being subtle and cautious. He had enough conceit about him to make a saint swear, Robin thought angrily. "I'm interested in seeing that my father isn't being taken for a ride! I'm interested in seeing that my beloved home county isn't turned into some kind of holiday camp because of some stupid town-hall planner who got sweet-talked by some clever up-country property developer! I'm interested in preventing the tranquility of at least one little bit of coastline from being swept away in the desire for a quick buck, to put it crudely!"

"Robin, really!" James's face had got progressively redder as his daughter's tirade gathered momentum, but to her surprise she saw that Luke wasn't in the least upset by her attack. He was openly grinning at her, as if it added spice to the whole proceeding to have the daughter of his new business partner so incensed by his proposals. The contracts had been signed, and Robin felt strongly that her father was signing his lifeblood away, and hers with it.

"It's quite all right, Mr. Pollard," Luke said easily. "This kind of thing happens all the time in our business. You can hardly blame your daughter for wanting to preserve the environment she loves. I find it highly commendable, and I can only suggest that you reserve judgment on me, Robin. Look over the plans for the development and come to the site with us tomorrow to see for yourself that it will all be done tastefully and won't resemble a holiday camp in the least. Please don't jump to conclusions before you see what's planned."

His coaxing voice made her wild with anger. She didn't want him reassuring her so condescendingly. She didn't want him "understanding" her in that patronising manner. She didn't want him there at all. She wished he'd never come. She wished he would go away and things could be as they had been before.

But Robin knew that was an impossibility. Her life had begun to change direction six weeks earlier. She had come home to Cornwall then, seeking a haven, finding the calm she sought. But she was too young and resilient to be in retreat for very long, and already she had begun seeking a new challenge, however subconsciously. It was time to begin living again.

And then Luke Burgess had come into her life. As yet, Robin didn't know just how much he was going to shape her destiny. There was only one thing of which she was certain: Whether she loved him or hated him, she could never be unaware of him. For Robin, at least, things could never be as they were before, for he had awakened the woman in her.

Chapter Three

Robin found it hard to sleep that night. Luke Burgess's face kept getting in the way whenever she closed her eyes. She had never met a man who had had such an instant effect on her, whether to irritate her or . . . Against her will she began to imagine the hardness in that face softened into tenderness . . . to imagine how it would be to be held by him, kissed by him, loved by him.

Robin moved restlessly beneath the thin bedclothes, which were in a tangle around her body. She thrust them away from her, knowing that the sudden heat that suffused her came from an inner source rather than the warmth of the night.

For breathless moments she allowed herself to dream. With her golden looks Robin had never lacked boyfriends, but there had never been one to stir her the way Luke Burgess did. She had never felt the adrenaline flow in her blood so searingly before, nor believed that the magnetic attraction between a man and a woman could be so overpowering or so instantaneous.

She tried to think clearly. There hadn't been any attraction that afternoon when the dark shadow of the man had spoiled her sunbathing. Yet, even then, with the sunlight glinting around Luke's dark head, she had been aware of some devil's touch, had known from that moment that he was a man who would have an appeal for women, even if Robin Pollard was the one who got away.

Right now she was beginning to wonder if she was going to be that lucky—if luck was the right word to use. To think of Luke in that context meant she was halfway to falling in love with him, and that was so absurd she wouldn't even give it a second thought. Damn the man, Robin thought angrily. She thumped her pillow into shape and closed her eyes, pushing him out of her mind with a superhuman effort.

The next morning she dressed casually in linen slacks and a white silk shirt that was smart enough for lunch at a hotel in Helston, yet casual enough for clambering about the hillside, inspecting the site for the new development.

"All ready for the fray?" James greeted her when it was time to leave for the half-hour drive into town through narrow lanes lined with hedgerow and overhanging trees tinged with autumn.

"You have an odd way of referring to it," Robin commented. "I thought you were all for this great new development scheme. Not having any doubts, are you, Dad?"

"I am not! I got the distinct impression that you and Luke were ready to do battle at every opportunity, though." James smiled slightly as he drove expertly through familiar byways, avoiding the late tourists enjoying the Indian summer.

"I'm sorry about all that," Robin muttered. "He just got me on the raw, that's all."

"So I gathered. Don't let your quick tongue run away with you, will you, darling? I'm quite happy about Luke's offer and confident about his integrity. I assure you I'm not being taken for a ride, as you so eloquently put it last night. Give me credit for having some business sense still. The fact that I'm retired from the rat race doesn't mean my brain has stopped working."

"Okay, Dad, you've made your point."

"So do us all a favor and try not to clash with Luke every time you meet, will you?" James went on relentlessly.

He really was concerned, Robin thought. It didn't matter anyway, because she was unlikely to meet Luke too often. For starters, she would make a point of keeping away anytime she knew he'd be down there.

Her resolve was cheering but a little premature. It implied that she had somewhere else to go, an interesting job to keep her occupied and new people to meet. And she had none of those things. Not yet. She had the whole of England in which to search for them, and her next resolve was to buy the national newspapers and see if anything suitable was being offered.

By the time James stopped the car in the small car park of the Helston Hotel, Robin felt she was on a more even keel. She loved this small Cornish town. When she was a child and her mother was alive, her parents used to bring her down from Truro every May eighth for the traditional Furry Day, when all traffic was banned from the town for the day and old dances were performed. The children danced in and out of the houses, carrying garlands of flowers and led by fiddlers. Later in the day the older people—including the notables, dressed in morning dress and top hats—

would repeat the performance. It was pure carnival. But today Helston was its usual congested small-town self, with tourists and locals vying for room.

They found Luke and Bill in one of the small lounges, both looking businesslike with folders and briefcases beside them. They all shook hands formally, and this time Robin almost snatched her hand away from Luke's, knowing she was being idiotic but not wanting to have a repeat performance of the sensuous palm-stroking of the day before. All the same, when the plans were spread out on a low table and Luke and Bill became crisp and businesslike, Robin couldn't help noticing his hands.

The fingers were long and tapering—what her mother used to call a pianist's hands. Mrs. Fowler would have approved, Robin thought inanely. The nails were clipped short and neat, and the backs of the hands were covered with fine dark hair. Each time he stretched out his arm to point out a new feature of the architectural drawings, Robin saw muscles rippling under his tanned skin.

Why didn't he wear a long-sleeved shirt like Bill? she thought crossly, and in the same instant asked herself why the hell it mattered anyway. But he disturbed her and she didn't want him to. It would have been easier on her if she could have found the man himself less physically attractive. She hated all he stood for, but she didn't exactly hate him, and the fact that she was drawn to him against her will made her temper shorter than usual.

"The holiday complex will be in full view from here." Robin stabbed a finger along the plans, where the cliffs jutted out into the sea.

Luke stared at her thoughtfully, knowing she was going to make every possible objection.

"Well, maybe so, but only the sea gulls will be getting a look," he said with elaborate patience. "And since I'm not planning on starting up a nature camp, I hardly think our clients will be too worried. People on holiday don't expect to be in total isolation, Robin."

"Some do."

"Then they won't choose to come here, will they? And despite your fears, this will be an exclusive development. The costs are pretty high, and we will attract only people who can pay."

"I see. So it's to be a hideaway for the filthy rich, is it?" Perversely, Robin managed to imply that naturally she expected to hear this. Luke would be in it for the money.

"Don't you think you're taking your objections a bit far, darling?" James Pollard said mildly. "I'm perfectly satisfied with the plans, and I must say I'm full of admiration at the way the complex will merge into the original environment."

And since it was her father's land, it didn't really matter a damn what Robin thought. There was no point in fighting it, except that it was in her nature to stick up for what she believed in. Right now she was making a stand for conservation and her own little space. She glared at Luke.

Hoping to ease the tension, Bill drew out some sketches from another folder and lay them down in front of her.

"This is the way it will look when all the work's finished, Robin. We discussed several different ideas and decided that low buildings with flat roofs, rather in the style of the Mediterranean complexes, would be best. We can keep the profile of the hillside virtually unchanged, and the white-painted villas would be an attractive feature among the trees."

"There aren't that many trees there."

"There will be," Luke said calmly.

Did he think he was God to go altering the landscape at will? But any hopes of changing their minds about this was fading quickly. It had obviously gone too far now, and her father had conveniently kept quiet about it all until Mrs. Fowler's death had forced Robin to come home. He was as much to blame as anyone. The entire male population was quickly going down in Robin's estimation—even the anxious-faced Bill, who was clearly not cut out to deal with irate females so early in the day.

"Just when is all this going to happen?" she asked next, her voice still frigid.

"We start work in two weeks," Luke informed her. "We will start moving in the heavy machinery at the end of next week, and the workmen will be installed in their temporary housing. I'm afraid there will be some disruption from noise for the next few months."

"How long will it take?" If it annoyed the neighbours enough, perhaps they could get up a petition. But there were very few neighbours except at Pollard Manor, and Robin guessed that any others would be compensated. She was reading Luke Burgess very well by now. He always got what he wanted. . . .

"I estimate that if we get a reasonable winter without too much rain we'll have the work done by Easter. We should be open for business for the early summer."

"I see. I shall be sure and find a job well away from home, then, while all the bulldozing is going on. Perhaps you'd better go to the Riviera for the winter, Dad."

"Like one of the filthy rich?" James grinned at her. "Now, why should I do that? This is as much my project as Luke's, only in a smaller way, of course. I'm very interested to see how it all develops, and I've no intention of skipping the country. Besides, since I'm to get a percentage of all the holiday bookings, don't you think I've a right to see that everything goes well? If there are any problems and the workmen need to get hold of Luke urgently, it will be useful to have a shareholder on the spot."

Robin gaped at him. This was news to her. James hadn't said anything about getting a percentage out of the holiday take. They really were business partners, then, even if Luke held most of the shares. Robin didn't like the thought of that one bit. He was infiltrating her life too quickly and smoothly.

"Do you have a job in mind, Robin?" Luke forced her to look at him. "Your father told us about your love of this part of Cornwall, and it must be good to relax after London. Are you planning on staying down here? I can't really believe you'd let me drive you away as you suggested just now."

His blue eyes challenged hers. She felt a tremor run through her body as their gazes locked. Why did he always manage to do this to her? She didn't want it—didn't want him. . . .

"You wouldn't," she said curtly. "I do as I please. I've never let any man dictate to me, not even Dad." She gave his hand a quick squeeze to let him know it wasn't he she was getting at. "I preferred working for a woman too. Mrs. Fowler and I understood each other perfectly. She had an artistic temperament."

"And yours is hardly predictable, is it?" Luke put in.

James gave a teasing laugh.

"You won't get the better of Luke, Robin. I get the feeling you're too much alike."

"Then, it's a good thing we won't be seeing too much of each other, isn't it?" she said.

Luke leaned back in the hotel chair, his long legs stretched out in front of him. He wore dark brown cord jeans and a cream shirt, and as he put his hands behind his head in a nonchalant gesture, Robin could see that there wasn't an ounce of spare flesh on him. He had a superb physique, and she grudgingly registered the fact. Any woman would fall for him, given half the chance, except for her. She saw him for what he was, an exploiter of people and the countryside. She wouldn't look beyond that.

"I was hoping we might see a great deal of each other, Robin," he went on, his eyes never leaving her face.

Robin's cheeks were tinged with colour, wondering suspiciously if his words were as innocent as they seemed. His expression mocked her, and then he sat forward, the businessman in him taking over.

"I have a proposition for you. I'm without a secretary at present and I need somebody quickly. I've had a couple of temps for the past few weeks, but they're all hopeless and usually go off in tears if I shout at them. I don't imagine you'd be quite as feeble as some of them."

"You're damn right I wouldn't," she said at once. "No man is worth getting into that kind of state for."

Luke ignored the jibe. "Will you take it, then?"

The conversation was getting away from her. Robin sat bolt upright now, her green eyes sparkling like gemstones.

"Work for you? Are you kidding?"

"I never joke about business. You'll realise that if you take the job. That's why I'm a success at thirty-two while other men of my age are still wet behind the ears. I own developments all over the country. I could buy up half of Cornwall and still have change in my pocket. I can buy anything I like."

The sheer arrogance of him left Robin speechless. That he had made a success of his business through ruthless contempt for anyone and anything else was flagrantly obvious to her. That he was making it insultingly plain that he fully intended buying her, too, if he couldn't have her any other way was also clear, to Robin if to no one else. Her father didn't seem to see it that way. Out of the corner of her eye Robin could see in her father's face nothing but admiration for a self-made man with plenty of style. Oh yes, he had style all right.

"Sorry, but it's no deal." Her voice was clipped, not trusting herself to say more.

Luke didn't let go as easily as that. "Think about it. You don't have to come to an instant decision. I'm offering a six-month contract with very favourable terms. If we suit each other after that time, we'll put it on a permanent basis. You'll find I'm a stickler for work, Robin, but there are compensations. For one thing, we'll be coming down here on site quite frequently. You'll be able to see your father more often than if you had a regular nine-to-five job in a London office. And Bristol isn't so far away. Think about it over lunch and while we're looking over the site this afternoon. Bill and I can stop over one more night if you decide you'll come back with us tomorrow."

Robin gasped. Apart from the suspicion about the "permanent basis" and the "compensations" he mentioned, did he really think she could decide on a new way of life as quickly as that? Robin brushed aside the fact that she was normally a creature of quick decisions and that part of the attraction of working for Mrs. Fowler had been the stimulation of sharing her life-style. Mrs. Fowler had long since given up playing the piano professionally on a strict tour basis, but she was still enough in demand to undertake occasional engagements, and Robin had enjoyed typing out the replies to the fan letters that still arrived, each one signed by Elaine Fowler herself.

But there was no way she was going to rush home and pack her things and go back to Bristol with Luke Burgess the next day. He must be mad to suggest it.

She stubbornly refused to comment any further, changing the conversation and talking directly to Bill and her father, totally ignoring Luke. It was almost time for lunch anyway, and all the plans and folders were put away as the four of them went into the hotel dining room. Only once more did Luke refer to his offer of employment, and then he spoke to James.

"Perhaps you'd persuade your beautiful daughter that I could really use her help, Mr. Pollard. Can't you put in a word for me?" The suggestion was half mocking, as if Luke had never really needed anyone to do anything for him.

James chuckled. "My daughter makes up her own mind, Luke, as you must have realised by now. And my guess is that she's already decided on her future."

Luke raised his glass towards Robin at that, as if to seal the bargain. Didn't he listen to anyone but himself? she wondered, bristling. From his expression everyone would assume that he had already got his way, and he certainly had not.

All the same, over lunch she let the idea mull around in her head. Would it be such a bad thing after all? At least she would know exactly what was going on at all stages of the development. Presumably she would have access to all the facts and figures of the project, and there would be no chance of Luke's putting one over on her father. Robin would know immediately if there was anything crooked about the deal. Not for one minute did she let the thought creep in that the chance to see more of Luke was too tempting to resist. It wasn't that at all. It certainly wasn't that!

After lunch they drove out to the site in separate cars, though at the last minute Luke had a suggestion to make.

"Perhaps you'd like to come with me, Robin, and I can explain a bit more about the project on the way, if we're going to be working together. . . ."

"I haven't said that we are."

"Bill can go with your father," he went on as if she hadn't spoken. "We'll meet up above the site."

James thought it was a good idea, so Robin had no option but to agree, unless she wanted to appear completely unreasonable. What was it about Luke Burgess? she thought savagely. He seemed to bring out the worst in her with no effort whatsoever.

They drove the first couple of miles in silence, and then Luke spoke softly.

"Why are you fighting me, Robin?"

"Why not? What did you expect? I've never been an active conservationist, but I know when the landscape is about to be desecrated by an ambitious land developer overkeen to line his own pockets." She deliberately misunderstood him.

"To hell with all that for the moment, though you're not stupid, my darling," he said lazily. "You know very well what I mean. Why do you fight the inevitable? The minute I saw you stretched out on that patch of sand, looking so deliciously sexy, I knew there was more to Cornwall than tales of piskies and smugglers. Any red-blooded man would have been stirred."

"I wasn't there for any male oglers," Robin snapped, her heart racing at the tone of his voice and the way his eyes kept leaving the narrow lane to glance over her body. She knew then that she had made a mistake: She should have insisted on riding with her father. She clamped her lips together, determined not to let him rile her. To her fury, his hand rested lightly on her thigh for a moment, the warmth of it penetrating her linen skirt. She jerked her leg away.

"Get this, Mr. Burgess"—she whipped her head round to glower at him—"women don't like being regarded as sex objects any more. We're liberated ladies these days, on equal terms with men, and if I am going to work with you, I want to make that very clear!"

"Good. That means you haven't entirely discarded the idea, then," he retorted. "And if you want to be treated as an equal, I don't have to soft-pedal anything I want to say to you, right? You can't have it both ways, Robin."

She looked at him suspiciously.

"I suppose so," she muttered. She didn't trust him.

The lane widened a little beneath a shady bower of trees and a little pull-in for cars. Luke suddenly turned the car into the side of the lane and pulled on the hand brake, leaving the engine running. Robin wasn't sure if it was the throb of the car engine or the uneven beat of her heart that was loudest as his arms came around her, imprisoning her in their embrace.

"Then I'll make it perfectly clear." Luke's face was very close to her own, and the tangy scent of fresh pine she'd noticed the day before drifted into her nostrils from his freshly shaven skin. He was so close that she could feel his heart against her breast, the thin fabric of their clothes doing little to lessen the effect of the contact. Robin knew a feeling of helplessness.

She should struggle. She should be outraged or unnerved by the desire she saw in his blue eyes, darkened with his need. She should fight against this. Hadn't he just been asking her why she continued to fight him? It wasn't in her nature to remain passive. She wasn't the clinging type, but incredibly she realised that she was almost clinging to Luke at that moment as her hands came up against his chest in a mute plea for him not to do that. . . .

His chest was hard and unyielding against her palms. In contrast Robin felt her soft female contours crushed to him. Her long silky hair fell back on her shoulders as one of Luke's hands gently caressed its golden tresses. It seemed to be an endless torment before his mouth took possession of hers, slowly at first, with a delicate pressure, and then more surely as he felt her instinctive response.

He was bruising her lips, forcing her mouth to open. His need to dominate was almost tangible, and she, who had never allowed any man to rule her, felt the strangely pleasurable feeling of submission sweep through her like a flame. Yet, it was not submission; it was a meeting halfway, an acknowledging of the senses and the flesh that made Robin feel exhilaratingly alive.

It was only the sound of another car passing them in the lanc that brought Robin back to awareness. Only then did she remember to struggle, to recall that this was the man who was disrupting a way of life. Luke still held her, his fingers digging into her slender shoulders for a moment, but he moved his mouth away from hers a fraction of an inch.

"Now try to deny that we're the same kind of people, you and I, Robin," he said huskily against her bruised lips. "We meet on equal terms, with the same needs, the same desires; your responses tell me you want me as much as I want you."

Robin pushed him away from her, sitting as far from him as she could in the car, her green eyes blazing.

"You're like all men," she lashed out at him. "You think all you have to do is turn on the sex appeal and women will grovel at your feet!"

"That wasn't quite what I had in mind." Luke grinned. "But maybe it wouldn't have worked after all. I'm not sure I could cope with a secretary with the looks of an angel and the temper of the devil. Let's forget the whole thing."

He released the hand brake and turned the steering wheel to get them back onto the road so suddenly that

Robin lurched against the door. Her eyes smarted at the sharp jab in her shoulder, but she wouldn't let him see it. She was too busy weighing the pros and cons of taking up the challenge of being Luke Burgess's secretary, weakly admitting to herself that the decision had already been made. The kiss had put the final seal on it.

Chapter Four

If she thought about it forever, Robin couldn't have said exactly how it happened that she came to be sitting in Luke Burgess's car the following morning, with most of her worldly goods packed into two suitcases, which were stuffed into the trunk of the car, along with Luke's and Bill's overnight bags. But it had happened, and she was going into what she still thought of as enemy territory in order to become Luke's secretary.

James had thought it a marvellous idea. He had a great admiration for Luke and never stopped telling Robin so. When they got back to Pollard Manor late the previous afternoon and she told her father that she had finally made up her mind, he had looked delighted.

"Does Luke know, or is this a sudden decision, darling?"

Robin had given a half-smile. She hadn't yet told Luke, but he knew all right. He was so damnably sure of her. To regain her crumbling self-respect, Robin had told herself firmly that she was only taking the job for one reason: to see that everything was aboveboard and that her father wasn't going to lose by going into business with Luke Burgess.

"I said I'd phone the hotel in Helston before six-thirty to give him my decision," she had said. "If I don't phone, he and Bill are going back to Bristol tonight. Otherwise, they'll stay on to give me time to pack."

Despite her doubts, Robin was thrilled that she was starting on a new kind of adventure—by which she meant the job, naturally. She had been with Elaine Fowler since leaving secretarial college, and it was strange to think of beginning all over again. She swallowed, trying to ease the tightness in her throat. The past was over, and regrets were pointless. It was a cynical philosophy, but one that had kept her grief under control in the sad days following Mrs. Fowler's death. She had needed all her strength then, and had only wilted upon coming home and collapsing into her father's understanding arms. Now, restored, Robin welcomed this new challenge.

She and Luke weren't quite on equal terms any more, either. In business, at least, Luke was now the boss. She admitted that much, but he'd find out that her subservience went only so far. The fact that she found him the most attractive, most intriguing, sexiest man she'd ever met had nothing at all to do with anything.

"I didn't expect this to happen so quickly," James had remarked as she began making frantic lists of what to take and what to leave behind, since she would be able to stay at the manor whenever they were on site—which was a big attraction of the job, Robin admitted. "You'll need to find somewhere to live."

She had already thought of that one, and gave a wry smile.

"I mentioned that, but you might have expected it to be no problem. Luke's not a property man for nothing. His last secretary left in a bit of a hurry, and her flat is ready and waiting for the next one to move in. It goes with the job."

Robin had bitten her tongue rather than ask why the last secretary had moved out so unexpectedly. She didn't want to know. If it was because the poor girl hadn't been able to handle Luke, then he'd learn that Robin was a very different proposition.

So there she was, right after lunch, heading out of Cornwall into Devon and onto the M5 motorway, which would take them to Bristol. By the time they crossed the Tamar River, which separated the two counties, Robin felt a strange shiver inside. They took the modern road bridge, but to the right of them was the twin-curved structure of Brunel's railway bridge spanning the river. For a crazy moment Robin thought that it seemed to symbolise her own life—leaving the old for the new—and who could tell her if she was making the right choice?

"Laying ghosts?" Luke prompted, after she had been silent for some time. Behind them, in the back seat, Bill dozed, and it felt as if there were only the two of them in the car. Robin shrugged. Until she actually began work in the office, they were still on equal terms, and she had always been one for speaking her mind.

"Just wondering if I'm making the biggest mistake of my life, that's all. Three days ago I had no intention of moving to Bristol. I've never even been there, apart from passing through by train. What am I doing here?"

She was talking to herself as much as to Luke. To her surprise she felt his hand covering hers for a few minutes until he needed to put it back on the wheel. For once, she wasn't tempted to snatch her own hand away. Instead she felt oddly comforted by the touch.

"You're doing me one hell of a favour, Robin, and when you get a look inside the office, you'll know why I'm paying you an excellent salary. Work has been piling up for two weeks since Maggie skipped off with her sailor, and you'll need to be a genius to unscramble some of the mess. That's why I asked you to take on the job. That—and other reasons . . ." he couldn't resist adding. "Don't you want to know what they are?"

"I'm not sure I do," Robin retorted. She wasn't taken in by false flattery, and so far Luke hadn't resorted to it, she realised with a little surprise. Not the usual kind that went with champagne and parties, anyway.

"I'll tell you all the same," he said calmly. "You're far more decorative than Maggie or any other girl I've had working for me, of course, but you're no doubt aware of that already. You must get bored with men telling you how beautiful you are, so I won't waste my breath in stating the obvious."

"Thank you," Robin said sarcastically, not sure how well she liked this line of approach. It was different! She did get suspicious of any man who came on too strong with the chat, but he didn't have to brush it all aside quite so curtly. A little finesse wouldn't have been unwelcome.

"You're also more intelligent than most."

Robin wasn't sure whether this was a particular compliment to her or a put-down of the rest of female society. She decided to let it pass without comment and looked stubbornly ahead at the ribbon of road in front of them.

"You've been suspicious of me ever since you heard about the holiday development, haven't you, Robin?

And I think you'd have been more convinced that I wasn't taking your father for a ride if I'd persuaded him to sell the land outright to me. You can't quite believe that I've made a fair and square business deal with him, can you? You can't believe that he'll get a reasonable percentage of the profits, though naturally it will be a far smaller percentage than my own."

By now Robin had jerked her head round to stare at him in furious embarrassment. It was true that she'd have felt easier if James had sold the parcel of land outright and had nothing more to do with it. She would have convinced herself it was because she wanted nothing to do with any holiday bungalow project . . . but Luke had seen the real reason. And since he knew . . .

"All right"—she became defensive—"so what if I did feel the need to protect my father's interests? Is that so strange?"

"Not at all. It's perfectly commendable. And when you know me a little better, I think you'll find that I'm quite trustworthy, Robin. I'm not a business shark."

There was a hint of laughter in his voice, and for a moment Robin felt at a loss for words. Then she muttered an ungracious apology, hardly knowing why she did so. She wasn't backing down from her opinion of Luke Burgess as a hard and arrogant man, but unless she could prove otherwise, she would give him the benefit of the doubt about his professional integrity. She was sure her father would have vetted him before signing a contract with him, and surely James was smart enough to recognise a charlatan.

"Forget it, Robin," Luke answered easily. "I just wanted to get one thing straight between us, that's all. You and I will be spending a good deal of time together in the next six months, and we don't have to start off as enemies."

"We're still on opposite sides, though, aren't we?"

"Are we?" Luke sounded mystified. "I thought you were on my side now, if that's the right way of putting it. In agreeing to work for me—"

"But you know the reason for that," Robin said sweetly. "To infiltrate the enemy camp, remember? You just told me so! I may have an angelic look, Luke, but I'm not gullible. And I prefer to form my own judgement of people."

"Just as long as you don't pre-judge. I seem to remember a delectable little spitfire absolutely sending me to hell with her eyes for moving into her personal space. Wasn't that the way you put it?"

"I didn't know who you were then. And it wouldn't have made any difference if I had." It was no good. The resentment was still there. She couldn't hide it.

Luke said nothing for a few minutes. When he spoke again his tone was a few degrees colder than before.

"How did such a charming man as James Pollard have a daughter like you? The outer covering might be pure honey, but it's solid rock inside, isn't it?"

Robin didn't answer. She knew that if she started, all the pent-up emotions she still hadn't fully unleashed since Mrs. Fowler's death would come rushing to the surface. Luke's words had caught her on the raw. Solid rock inside . . . if he only knew how vulnerable she felt at that moment. How badly she grieved for that charming lady, and how her generous heart was full to overflowing with this churlish man's assessment of her. Solid rock—she was never that.

Couldn't he see the effect of so much change in her life in so short a time? But why should he bother to understand how a woman felt? His type of man saw women in two contexts only—as underlings to work for them, or as bedmates. Thank God she had elected to be the former, Robin thought. He had made it plain that he desired her, but he felt only lust, not love. Robin doubted if Luke Burgess even knew the meaning of love.

It was a relief when Bill stirred from his dozing in the back seat, when the long stretch of motorway came to an end as Luke put on the left-hand indicator in the car and they moved on to ordinary roads again.

"I thought you'd like to cross another Brunel masterpiece," he said conversationally. "The Clifton suspension bridge over the river Avon. It looks better from a distance, really, especially when it's lit at night with strings of electric lights and looks very delicate. You'll be able to see it like that later."

Robin flexed her tired muscles. It had been a long drive; they had stopped only once for cups of tea at a service station. Luke paid the bridge toll and they cruised over the bridge, the narrow river winding its way through the Avon Gorge a dizzying distance below them. On the other side Luke turned left again, and they drove through roads bordered by wide green stretches of grass, with thickets of trees and elegant town houses in the background.

"Is this Bristol?" Robin said in surprise. "I expected it to be more congested with houses and buildings."

"Not this part. This is Clifton, where I live and where you'll be living too. Bill's car is parked at my place, so when we've let him out, I'll take you to your flat and you can get settled in."

It was suddenly all unreal. The thought of being dumped in a strange flat, in an unfamiliar city, among total strangers was beginning to tie her stomach in knots. She must have been crazy to agree to this. And once Bill had departed, she would be alone with Luke. She didn't want him around, but if he wasn't, she'd feel entirely on her own.

As if he knew exactly what was going through her mind, Luke's hand covered hers again for a brief instant.

"Don't worry, Robin, I won't abandon you until you've got your bearings," he said.

"Thanks. At the moment I feel a bit like a lamb being led to the slaughter," she muttered.

What was wrong with her? Where was the pioneering spirit that made her always eager for new experiences? For the moment it seemed to have deserted her, and tiredness was making her feel dull-witted. That was it, Robin thought. She was just tired, and once she was able to have a long soak in a fragrant bath, she would feel restored.

"Is there a phone in the flat, Luke?" she asked suddenly. "I want to call my father and let him know I've arrived."

"You'll find everything in working order, including the phone. Maggie was a notorious late sleeper and needed a regular call to get her to the office each day."

Robin wondered briefly just how friendly he had been with his former secretary. She had skipped off with a sailor, so the story went, but that didn't mean she and Luke hadn't been close before the sailor appeared on the scene. Not that it mattered to Robin. She couldn't care less how many women Luke had in his life, just as long as she wasn't included in the list.

She hadn't yet found the one man with whom she wanted to share her life . . . but when she did, Robin was very sure it had to be an exclusive relationship. Would Luke even consider that within his world of high-powered wheeling and dealing? And why was she even considering him as a candidate, anyway?

Before she could stop them, the sweet images were enveloping her. Had she ever known a man like Luke before—one who could storm his way into her life and set her aflame the way he did? Did the memory of any other man's kisses linger with erotic passion and tender warmth at the same time? Had she ever felt this disturbed by a stranger? If this was falling in love, then she didn't want to know about it.

"Oh, no"—the whispered words left her lips, and Luke glanced at her as he stopped the car outside an elegant house set back in tree-lined grounds, with the sweep of the Downs in front of it and a tantalising glimpse of the fairy-tale bridge to the left and in the distance. Luke's house.

"Did you say something, Robin?"

Bill was already getting out of the car and opening the trunk to get his overnight bag. Robin swallowed. She was appalled by the sudden realisation that her feelings for this man weren't quite what they had been in the beginning! She still hated what he stood for, but she was becoming irresistibly drawn to the man himself—and that was something she had no intention of admitting to anyone.

"I expected some modern futuristic place," she floundered inanely. Luke gave a short laugh.

"You mean you thought I'd have no taste, right? I can see your education regarding a dreaded property developer is far from complete. It will be my pleasure to change your way of thinking, Robin."

He didn't get out of the car or turn off the engine, and Bill didn't seem to expect it. The small car in the drive was clearly his, and he called out goodbye to the two of them as he moved towards it, saying he'd see them at the office the next morning. Luke's car moved off, to circle the verdant patch of Downs and stop outside another building almost directly opposite Luke's house.

"This is where you'll live, Robin. I had the place converted into flats a few years ago and kept the one on the top floor for my secretary. It has the best view, and there's a lift in case you can't cope with four flights of stairs. Come on, I'll take you inside."

Robin got out of the car, feeling as if none of this was really happening. She watched Luke take her luggage from the trunk and followed him up the stone steps to the big front door. There was a spacious hall inside and he went at once to the lift and loaded the suitcases inside. *Like a lamb to the slaughter* . . . Robin couldn't get the ridiculous phrase out of her head. Suddenly she couldn't think of a single thing to say to him as they rode silently upwards in the closeness of the lift. Close—yet there was a sudden distance between them. She was his employee and his tenant, and the feeling of awkwardness she was experiencing annoyed her. She felt so tense, as if she would snap in two if he tried anything now.

Luke unlocked the door of the flat and stood aside for her to go in. It was very tastefully furnished and clean and had an excellent view. She could see Luke's house and the Clifton suspension bridge. At night it would be beautiful.

Luke spoke abruptly. "I'll leave you to browse around and unpack, Robin. It's just after six now. I'll be back at eight, and we'll have dinner together. You won't want to be on your own on your first evening here."

He handed her a key, and before she could reply he had turned on his heel and was gone. Robin looked out the window. When he was outside the building and getting back into his car, Luke looked up for a moment and raised his hand in salute. Robin waved back and watched him drive off. Such a little distance to go, yet she felt idiotically as if she were being deserted.

How stupid she was being! Angry at herself, Robin moved away from the window and looked quickly around the flat. It was very nice indeed, with one large bedroom and a smaller one; a bathroom; a tiny kitchen and a pleasant lounge. It was impersonal at the moment, needing the stamp of someone's personality on it to bring it to life. Her brain worked quickly, not letting her uncertainty take control. Photographs and records and books—she had had the foresight to bring some with her, and once they were unpacked . . .

But first she would phone her father. Hearing his familiar voice would help to make her feel less disoriented. Robin dialled the number and relaxed a little as she told him she was fine and the flat was lovely, and that she'd call him again the following night to let him know how she'd got on at the office. And as James was going out for the evening, Robin didn't prolong the call. The small contact was gone.

A bath. That would be next. Unpack some of her clothes and unwind. Her thoughts seemed to jerk through her head in staccato bursts. She was more alone than she had ever really been since Elaine Fowler's death. She was without the hectic work load that had been thrust upon her at that time, away from the cocoon of her father's sympathy for her distress over someone he had never met. Alone.

This was feeble, Robin told herself angrily. She pulled her toilet bag out of one suitcase, and a simple blouse and skirt and a change of underwear from the other. She couldn't think properly, and she was disgusted with herself. It was totally unlike her.

Ten minutes later, soaking in the soft fragrance of a soothing bath, some of the tension lifted fractionally. She told herself she was at the start of a new adventure, and Robin had never been one to balk at new experiences. She welcomed them. She was foolish to let the ghosts of the past drain all her energy. Besides, she needed all her wits about her to deal with Luke Burgess and to assure herself that he really was all he said he was.

She even found herself humming a little tune as she dressed and applied fresh makeup. She was fond of the blouse she wore; it was a rich plum colour and went well with her beige skirt. It gave her confidence and made her feel good. She had no idea where she would be dining with Luke, and it was suitable for just about anywhere. Robin began looking round the flat with a feminine interest. There was a TV and even a record player in the lounge. On impulse Robin riffled through the collection of LPs she'd brought and put one on the turntable. The well-remembered strains of one of Elaine Fowler's most frequently requested melodies seemed to fill the room. Robin sank down on the settee as the lovely haunting tune of *Plaisir d'Amour* washed over her. She closed her eyes, seeing in her imagination the white-haired, straight-backed lady who had played the tune, her long fingers seeming to caress the keys.

One second Robin was dreaming wistfully, caught up in the music and days that were gone; the next she was hugging a cushion to her breast in a paroxysm of weeping, crying her heart out in a way she had been unable to do until now. There seemed to be no end to her crying—it racked her whole body, blinding her to everything but the need to express her grief physically. For once, she didn't want to be the strong one, the capable one.

She didn't hear the knock on the door of the flat, nor did she notice when the knocking was repeated. She wasn't aware of a key being inserted in the lock, or of someone entering the lounge, or of troubled eyes looking down at her.

Her heart leapt when she realised that someone was taking the cushion gently away from her. She looked up and saw the blurred shape of Luke blocking her line of vision as he had done the first time she saw him. Then she had been angry with him. Now she could only look mutely, her heart still thudding at his unexpected appearance, her cheeks flushed, her golden hair a tangle of confusion. If she had even cared to think about it, she would have thought that she looked a mess.

But she didn't think of it, and neither did he. With one soft, expressive oath, he pulled her gently to her feet and folded her in his arms, holding her against his chest as if to let his own strength flow into her.

"Cry your tears for her, baby." His voice was gentle in her ear. "You're a crazy woman, pretending to be harder than you really are. Women aren't meant to be tough. Your Elaine Fowler wasn't, was she? Anyone who can play the piano with such sensitivity must have been a caring person, and she'd be glad to know that Robin Pollard is still capable of weeping, despite her sophisticated veneer. Let it happen, darling."

The words flowed over her like music. She wept against him, oblivious to the fact that she was spoiling the clean shirt he'd just put on. She felt safe and warm and wanted. And when the bout of crying had lessened a little, she was even able to whisper into his shoulder and attempt a thin joke.

"I thought I was supposed to be solid rock. How do you know which is the real me, Luke?"

He looked down into her misty eyes. She couldn't see the expression in his since he stood against the light and the night was already turning the sky outside to a soft velvet blue.

"I'm not sure yet. But we have plenty of time to find out, don't we, Robin?"

The faint touch of arrogance, of the Luke she knew, was back in his voice. For a moment the old antagonism trembled between them, and then his mouth was seeking hers in a long sweet kiss and she was locked in his embrace, melting against him, the hidden fire of passion muted, yet as undeniable as the night. Robin knew that this was the only place she wanted to be at that moment. It was all she needed, to be held and comforted like that.

The record ended, and the lilting strains of the music faded away. But the music was all in her head now . . . *Plaisir d'Amour,* the pleasures of love . . . the pleasures of love. And what she was experiencing now in Luke's arms was surely one of them.

Chapter Five

Carefully, Robin extricated herself from Luke's arms. For blissful moments it had seemed the haven of her dreams, but as reality intruded with the ending of the piano music on the record, she became acutely embarrassed by the situation. She tried so hard to appear cool and efficient—which was what she assumed Luke Burgess would need in a secretary, after all—and there she was, within such a little time, proving herself to be vulnerable. Now that she was no longer so highly emotional, the memory of the touch of arrogance in Luke's voice superseded all other thoughts. She gave a shaky laugh and turned her face away from him to hide the heat in her cheeks.

"I'm sorry. I don't usually behave like that in front of a stranger."

"I thought we'd progressed beyond all that 'stranger' nonsense." He was as forthright as ever, his previous gentleness gone. It was easier on her, she thought, with a sighing breath. She could cope with him when they struck sparks off each other. When he became protective, caring, her bones seemed to crum ble, her self-sufficiency to vanish. Her short laugh was stronger this time.

"Don't cash in on the situation, Luke," she made herself say lightly. "You know very well I'm still grieving for someone I loved as a friend as well as an employer, and I think you know very well why I agreed to take on this job."

"Can't you forget the job for one minute?" he said angrily. "You're not a work machine, and I wouldn't want you to be one. Were you so coolly standoffish with Elaine Fowler, I wonder?"

He had moved round to face her, and she couldn't prevent the hot tears from springing to her eyes. She blinked them away angrily.

"That's not fair." Her voice vibrated unsteadily.

"No, it's not," he said calmly. "But you know the boring old cliché: 'All's fair in love and war.'"

"This must be war, then. It's certainly not love," Robin retorted before he could make any more platitudes. She didn't want to hear them. Her stomach was churning because of the upheaval of the last ten minutes. It had been a long day, ending with an entirely new situation, and what was more, she was suddenly very hungry. She recognised the gnawing feeling with something like relief, and brought the conversation down to basics. "I thought you said something about dinner, or do you always drive your employees to the brink of starvation before you feed them?"

Luke stared thoughtfully into her glowing eyes—which were at that moment as wild as the Cornish sea—and saw that she had had enough. He leaned forward unexpectedly and touched his lips to hers, so lightly that it was no more than a brushing of his skin against her own, an expression of tenderness without passion, but memorable for all that. Nothing he did went unregistered in her mind, Robin realised anew. It was an inescapable fact.

"Let's go, then."

"You'll have to wait while I patch up my face. I can't go anywhere looking like this."

"You only have to walk across the Downs. We're eating at my place, and before you start going all Victorian on me, it's perfectly respectable. My housekeeper lives in, and she's looking forward to meeting you. Now, go and dab your face, and let's move. Mrs. Somerton's not the type to think the worst at our nonappearance, but it would be a shame to let her excellent cooking spoil."

Robin went quickly to the bathroom to sponge her face with cold water, feeling all kinds of an idiot. Luke's words made her feel naive, and she hated him for producing the feeling in her. She had met all kinds of people while working with Elaine Fowler, and she considered herself a pretty good judge of character. Robin could immediately pick out rakes or roués, to use Mrs. Fowler's old-fashioned terms.

They might be old-fashioned names, but the intentions of the men who earned them hadn't altered through the ages. Luke wasn't one of them, but he had the ruthless male charisma of a successful man who combined wealth with good looks and sex appeal. He was one of a kind. Luke Burgess might epitomise many things that she despised and mistrusted, but he was still unique. That was what made him doubly dangerous as far as she was concerned, and she was more vulnerable than she had thought.

She applied fresh makeup. Her eyes still looked less clear than usual, and her cheeks were flushed, but there was no helping it. Maybe the cool air outside would restore some of her serenity. Unfortunately there wouldn't be much of it, since Luke's house was only a stone's throw away, and she shrugged resignedly. When she returned to the lounge, Luke was gazing out of the window. For a moment Robin felt her heartbeat quicken. His face was in profile and his expression unguarded, the frequently taut muscles in his face relaxed. Crazily, Robin had the fleeting sensation that he was a lonely man, for all his wealth and business success, a man still lacking the one element vital to his happiness—the perfect partner with whom to share his life.

Foolishly she pushed the feeling aside as Luke turned to her, and she decided she must have imagined the odd little lost look on his face. He inspected her with a professional eye and nodded.

"You'll do," he said briskly. "You'd better bring a jacket. It's quite cool, and I thought we'd take a walk over the Downs after dinner to let you get the feel of the place."

As if she wasn't entirely exhausted, Robin thought grimly! Emotion was as tiring as a ten-mile hike, and she seemed to be getting her share of it lately, whether it was tearful or explosive. But a walk after dinner might be preferable to any late-night tête-à-tête, and she agreed at once. Luke was still smiling as they left the flat and walked the short distance to his house, just as if he could read her mind—and if he could, she just didn't care.

Luke's house was an agreeable surprise, not ultra-modern or furnished extravagantly, but a comfortable home. The fittings were naturally expensive, as was to be expected, but unobtrusively so. The carpets were thick and plain, the walls liberally hung with paintings and grouped family photographs, which was oddly endearing, especially when he told her that none of his family was living. It contrasted with the way Robin had expected a property magnate's home to be, though she couldn't really have said why she'd formed such an impression of the breed.

She immediately liked Mrs. Somerton, a woman in her sixties, who obviously thought the world of him. One point in his favour, Robin conceded. There was a Mr. Somerton, too, who attended to the outside of the house and saw that things ran smoothly while Luke was away. Old family retainers, in effect. She hadn't considered his home life at all, and it was one more surprising facet of Luke's character. If she had considered it, she might have thought he lived in hotels or had a team of whiz-kids surrounding him. It was just as she had thought before: She didn't know him at all.

"What are you looking so quizzical about?" His voice came softly to her over the candlelit dinner table, and she realised that she had been staring at his strong-boned face—staring without really seeing—and now she felt her cheeks flush.

"I was just envying you such a super lady as Mrs. Somerton," she lied. "That was a delicious meal, and the most wonderful chocolate meringue—"

"It was, and I agree, but you were thinking no such thing," he cut across her words. "Your thoughts were far more personal, I suspect. A penny for them, Robin."

"Oh—"

"What is it?" Luke asked quickly, his blue eyes demanding the truth. Robin felt her composure slipping away and fought to regain it.

"I'm being so stupid tonight. It must be the long drive and the strangeness of everything. I'm not normally like this, Luke. It was just that phrase, 'A penny for your thoughts.' I must have heard it a thousand times in my life. It's just that Mrs. Fowler always used to say it when she thought I was getting worried about something, and it—it took me by surprise, that's all. You must think me feeble. You'll be regretting you ever took me on." She fumbled for the tissue she'd tucked up her sleeve, missing the tender look that crossed his face.

"No I won't. And I don't think you feeble at all. I think you're a perfectly normal young woman. What makes you think you have the right to be superior to anyone else?"

Robin looked at him in astonishment, his calm reply checking the new rush of emotion.

"I don't follow you. I don't think I'm superior to anyone."

"Yes you do. You think it's somehow shameful to allow yourself to grieve for someone you loved. Why should Robin Pollard be such a superior being that she can't do what ordinary mortals do and break down and weep now and then? It's perfectly natural that remembering a particularly poignant moment, hearing someone's favourite remark, or listening to their music, should move us to tears. Grief needs time, just like any other human emotion. When you love someone deeply, it's an insult to their memory to gloss over your private pain at losing them."

Robin felt her mouth drop open at his little speech. It pulsated with suppressed passion, yet it was delivered in a wholly detached way. Intuitively, Robin guessed that Luke, too, had lost someone very dear to him. She ran her tongue over her dry lips, knowing she couldn't ask.

"That was quite a lecture," she said shakily. "I hadn't expected you to be quite so—so perceptive."

He laughed, but there was little mirth in the sound.

"Oh, I assure you that even we hardheaded business tycoons can be capable of some finer feelings. Now, if you've finished your coffee, how about that walk? Do you feel up to it?"

"Yes, please—and thank you, Luke."

"You're welcome. I'll pass your thanks on to Mrs. Somerton. She's the one who deserves them."

She hadn't been thanking him for dinner, and he knew it, but the evening had become too highly charged to pursue it. Luke fetched her jacket and held it out for her, his hands lingering on her shoulders for a moment as she slipped her arms into it. She felt his warm breath against her hair. She thought he intended to kiss her, to twist her into his arms and capitalise on the moment, and the thought was suddenly unbearable. She felt as brittle as glass and moved swiftly away from him.

"Let's make it a short walk, though, shall we? I'm desperately tired, and I wouldn't want to be late on my first morning at work."

"That's fine by me. I have a pile of correspondence to go through tonight anyway." He was instantly remote. "I'd better vet it all before I hand it over to you at the office. Some letters can be quite abusive."

He was steering her towards the door now, and she felt a stab of irritation as they went out into the cooler night air and the soft blanket of darkness.

"Good Lord, do you think me incapable of handling a few abusive letters? I'm not some fragile plant, Luke, and I won't faint at the sight of a few expletives!"

"Good. I never expected that you would," he said.

Later she remembered the note of satisfaction in his voice and wondered if he'd goaded her a little into a stinging reply in order to discharge some of the tension between them. It was odd to think of Luke as a bit of a psychologist, but whether he had intended to or not, he had taken the heat out of the situation.

The walk across the springy turf of the Downs was exhilarating, and the view of the silvery river Avon far below in the gorge was breathtaking and unreal. The suspension bridge was a tracery of fairy lights, adding to the illusion of unreality. They walked for half an hour, by which time Robin was more than ready for bed, and Luke left her at the entrance of her new home with no attempt to prolong the moment.

"I'll call for you at nine-fifteen in the morning," he said. "There's no point in trying to fight the city traffic any earlier. Good night, Robin. Sleep well."

"Good night." He was already striding towards the stretch of green that separated their two establishments, a tall, dark, shadowy figure, soon swallowed up in the night. Again Robin felt that Luke was a very solitary person, which was probably ludicrous.

Her tiredness was making her see things that weren't there and blurring the edges of reality. She forcibly reminded herself that Luke was the enemy invading her territory, her special place in Cornwall. But as she gave her face a token cleansing and brushed her teeth before tumbling into bed, her final drifting thoughts were that even the concrete jungle of a city could be beautiful when seen with someone special. She forgot that so far she had only seen the green and verdant areas and the points of historical interest. She was too tired to think any more, sinking pleasurably into a welcoming cocoon of sleep, able to disregard completely the unfamiliarity of her surroundings.

When Luke arrived for her next morning, she was downstairs, in the foyer of the building. He expressed mocking surprise at her promptness, remarking that she was a vast improvement on Maggie in one respect at least.

"Thank you," she replied. She swung her legs inside the car, refusing to let him irk her. It was a sparkling morning, and after a good night's sleep Robin felt refreshed and ready to face the day with a keenness she hadn't felt in some weeks. The prospect of being in the business world again, whether it was Luke Burgess's business or not, was more reviving than she had realised. As Luke's car gathered speed and skirted the lush green of the Downs, she saw that they were in the highest part of the city, and as she looked down she saw spread out before her a mass of buildings that were a bewildering mixture of old and new. To someone like Luke the cloisterlike aspect of the older parts of the city must grate, and she commented as much. He nodded, never taking his eyes from the road as they moved even nearer to the business district some distance away.

"Bristol was badly blitzed during the war," he told her. "Town planning isn't always what the purists would like, and necessity comes before aesthetics when people are homeless. People must be given shelter, whether it's hastily built, prefabricated homes or great impersonal blocks of flats."

"I gather neither is to your liking." She was in total agreement with him there.

"Hardly, but I wasn't in the business of house-building at that time."

"I never thought I'd hear you call yourself a house-builder," she said, amazed to realise that she was almost teasing. Luke shrugged.

"When you bring my profession down to basics, that's all it is, Robin. It doesn't do to get too impressed with yourself in this life."

She bit back the retort that Luke could have fooled her. There were times when he could be startlingly introspective, and that intrigued her. It sometimes seemed that the brash tycoon wasn't really him at all, not the real Luke Burgess. He had said something similar about her. Maybe everyone played a part in front of other people . . . maybe with a hundred different parts. It was a thought that had never struck

Robin before. Who would he be today? she wondered. It would be interesting to see him with his office staff. It had been quite revealing to see him with Mrs. Somerton the night before, she recalled. There had been a real affection between them, and the older woman had treated Luke as someone between an employer and a well-loved nephew. There was certainly more to Luke than she had originally thought if he could produce such strong feelings in whoever knew him, feelings of loyalty or aggression. . . .

The car was drawing up in the parking space marked STAFF outside a huge glass and concrete building, and Luke grinned at her as he switched off the engine.

"Does this match your idea of a tycoon's office?" he asked. "Slick enough for you, is it?"

"It's what I expected." Robin was noncommittal, not wanting him to guess how much he was filling her thoughts. And he did dominate her thoughts, she admitted uneasily. It was probably natural, since she didn't as yet know anyone else there except Bill Withers, but it would be good to meet some more people and dismiss the unwanted notion that Luke Burgess could soon become an obsession.

The offices of Burgess Developments were on the fourth floor. They were plush, light and airy. There was a junior secretary, who spent most of her time filing her nails or making tea for visitors, and there was a receptionist whom Robin liked at once. Her name was Maureen, and once Luke had introduced her, he glanced at his watch and said he'd be back later that afternoon.

"Maureen will show you the ropes, Robin. Most of your work this morning will be dealing with the correspondence I looked over last night. I've put notes at the margins for replies, and I'm sure you can see to it. Leave it all out for my signature when I get back, and if there are any queries, we'll sort them out then. Look after her, Maureen. She's special."

"Aren't they all!" Maureen said darkly, as Luke blew them both a kiss and disappeared out of the door. The clean tang of his aftershave went with him, and Robin felt lost for a moment. She had expected him to be showing her around personally and was a little piqued that he hadn't done so. She didn't intend to let Maureen see that, though, but she noted Maureen's remark with a little tightening of her stomach. Wasn't it just as she had thought from the minute she saw Luke gazing down at her on her beach, with the sunlight framing his head? The typical male chauvinist. . . .

She realised that Maureen was smiling at her with something like relief and forced herself to pay attention.

"I was so glad when Luke phoned to say we had a new secretary on the way," she said chattily. "Things have been pretty chaotic since Maggie left, and Sonia's worse than useless. Where did he find you so quickly?"

Robin felt her cheeks colour. Put into words, it sounded very different from the usual method of finding employment.

"My father is James Pollard. You may have heard of him."

"The guy Luke's doing business with in Cornwall?"

"That's right." Robin kept the smile fixed on her face. "I happened to be without a job at the moment, so when Luke offered me this post, I decided to take it."

It sounded awful. Even as she spoke Robin knew she gave the impression of someone who didn't really need a job, flitting in and out of whatever position took her fancy. Fortunately, Maureen didn't seem to see it that way.

"Lucky you. It must have been a red-letter day when you saw Luke. Dishy, isn't he? Though I don't suppose you've ever had any trouble finding a boyfriend." Her look was filled with cheerful envy.

"I don't think of Luke as my boyfriend. He's my employer!"

"Well, I know, but stranger things have happened, and it was easy to see he fancied *you.* I saw that right away. Of course, I know the signs by now. . . ."

Robin felt hot all over. "Hadn't you better tell me what I'm supposed to be doing this morning, Maureen?" she asked pointedly. She certainly didn't want to stand there and discuss Luke Burgess, especially when Maureen was confirming all she had first thought about the man. If Maureen knew him well enough to read all the signs, there must have been plenty of women in his life. And Robin Pollard had no intention of being added to his list of conquests. It was bad enough that he was taking up her space at home; she must not allow him to invade her heart as well.

"Do you want coffee or tea?" Sonia asked Robin in a bored voice as the latter sat behind the desk in her office, before what seemed a mountain of paperwork. Sonia looked as if she'd be more at home in a disco than a property developer's office. Robin glanced at her watch. She'd been there all of ten minutes.

"Already?"

"I have to go out for Mr. Burgess in half an hour. It's the way I've always done things around here."

"That's fine," Robin said hastily. She didn't want to be the one to make waves. She didn't intend working there forever anyway. It was just an interim arrangement. It suited her on two counts: She could keep an eagle eye on what exactly Luke was doing with her father's property, and it eased her over the sense of loss after Elaine Fowler's death.

She gave Sonia a bright smile. "I'll have coffee,

please, and perhaps you'd have time to show me the filing system before you go, Sonia."

"All right." The appeal to the girl's superior knowledge of office routine obviously worked, and she was noticeably less prickly by the time she went out on Luke's errands.

By then Robin had got the desk in some sort of order. It had needed only a methodical approach and a bit of time and organisation. She had an In tray and an Out tray, and knew exactly what was pending and what needed urgent attention.

Several clients came and went during the morning. Bill Withers looked in to collect some papers and was clearly pleased to see Robin installed. Farther along the corridor, in another office, Roy Hutchings, the chief architect, introduced himself to Robin about mid-morning; he was a middle-aged, rather intense man whom she liked at once.

Maureen perched on the edge of Robin's desk and suggested that they both go to a nearby cafe for lunch.

"Unless you've any other plans, of course."

"No, I haven't." Robin was grateful to her, her thoughts not having progressed that far. Maureen locked the office once they were all ready to leave, and she and Robin went out together. The cafe was just along the road, in the middle of a small row of shops, and Maureen said they made delicious pizza. They both settled on that, and Robin spoke casually while they waited.

"How long have you worked for Luke, Maureen?"

"Oh, about two years now. He's a great boss. He doesn't worry you as long as the work gets done, and he's lavish with presents at Christmas and birthdays. Everybody falls for him, of course." Her plump face went a little dreamy and then she grinned. "Fat chance I'd have of a romantic interlude with Luke, when he could have his pick of the Miss World contestants!"

"I suppose he has plenty of girl friends." She was fishing, and she knew it.

Maureen laughed. "Dozens, love. Well, with his looks, and his money—" She suddenly realised that Robin was genuinely curious, and she put a warning note into her voice. "I'd say it won't be long before he gets amorous with you, Robin. You're just the type to intrigue our Luke: cool and classy, yet you've still got an outdoor look about you. And those green eyes! They're really beautiful. But don't let him fool you, Robin. He always says that love 'em and leave 'em is his motto, so Lord help the girl who's looking for wedding bells!"

Robin's smile was a little forced at this crisp analysis of Luke's character. "Not every girl is these days," she said lightly.

"You're right there," Maureen agreed. She looked at Robin shrewdly. "I'd say you weren't the sort to go in for casual affairs, Robin. Something tells me it's marriage or nothing for you, and if I'm right, I'd steer clear of a certain person's advances if I were you!"

The pizzas arrived, saving Robin from having to give any sort of answer. It was just as well, because she wasn't at all sure what kind of answer she could give.

Chapter Six

It took Robin very little time to settle into the office routine and into her new life. Being in close contact with Luke when he was in the office meant she learned very quickly that all his dealings were apparently strictly aboveboard. He wasn't in the habit of undercutting business rivals or buying up valuable pieces of land at rockbottom prices unless they were offered to him at such prices. He paid a fair price and was highly respected by clients and associates alike.

Robin was forced to concede that in business, at least, there was nothing for which she could readily condemn him. Dealing with invoices for building materials of all kinds, she admitted, too, that there was nothing of the cowboy about him. Materials were of the best quality, and property with Luke Burgess's name on it was guaranteed.

If she were any other secretary working for such a boss, she would have counted herself lucky. As it was, there was still the undeniable fact that the holiday complex Luke was building in Cornwall was on part of her territory, and he had no right to be there. She freely admitted she was unreasonable about it. She didn't want the tourists there. She didn't want Luke there, and the resentment towards him and her father for allowing him to build didn't lessen.

As for the man himself, in the weeks that followed, Robin was forced to admire his business sense. Often she had to answer letters from enthusiastic clients and listen to glowing remarks about his integrity. His staff, too, was loyal. Even Maureen's unguarded remarks over lunch that first day had been made with tolerant affection. If Maureen were ever accused of gossiping, she would have been truly horrified.

There was definitely something about the man, Robin admitted grudgingly. And something else intrigued her too. Far from bombarding her with his attentions, Luke had been oddly reticent about asking her out. On several occasions he'd taken her to dinner at some of the city's best restaurants. Once they'd gone to a restaurant on a ship in the river, and they'd taken a drive one Sunday afternoon out to the Mendip Hills and the coast. Apart from that, he'd made no attempt to seek her out.

Robin was alternately relieved and annoyed. After Maureen's warning, she had bristled a little whenever Luke was around, expecting to get the big macho treatment, but it didn't happen. She was suspicious, wondering if he was doing this deliberately, allaying her earlier hostility with a calculated display of charm. Finally, one afternoon when he had suggested that she go with him to view a new site and she was alone in the car with him as they sped out of the city towards the open country, Robin could contain her curiosity no longer.

"Have I got two heads or something lately, Luke?"

she demanded, in what her father used to call her bossy voice. "You seem very distant towards me. I hope my work is satisfactory."

They were in open farmland now, at the top of a rise. Far below, Robin could see the foundations and iron girders of the country club being erected, and a small team of workmen who looked like ants. Luke stopped the car at a good vantage point. The windows were halfway down, and the clean, fresh air was like wine. Without the noise of the engine to distract them, she was suddenly aware of the total silence all around them. They might have been the only two people in the world. There was only one sound she was registering, and that was the pounding of her heart, loud as thunder in her ears as Luke turned to her. His voice was soft and slightly thick.

"I've no complaints about your work, Robin." He dismissed the thought like tossing away unwanted rubbish. "I've no complaints about anything regarding you. I thought I'd made that perfectly obvious from the minute I saw you."

"That's all right, then." She gave a shaky laugh and ran her tongue round her lips, which were suddenly dry. Like a mouse caught in a trap, the thought ran around her head that they were miles from anywhere, and there was the sudden dark gleam in Luke's eyes that hadn't been noticeable lately. But it was there right now, and so was the triumphant smile playing around his sensual mouth. She wouldn't look at it.

He leaned towards her. His finger traced the curve of her cheek with a gossamer touch, sending little shivers of awareness through her. It trailed beneath her chin, stroking lightly, delicately, and Robin thought frantically that if he didn't stop, she would scream. One sensitive finger stroking the skin could be unbelievably erotic.

His eyes challenged her to jerk away, but if she did, then he would know just how his touch was affecting her. She stared into his eyes unblinkingly and heard him give a soft laugh.

"You may sit there with that frigid look on your face, Robin, but those expressive eyes of yours tell me something different. Whoever said the eyes are the windows of the soul knew what he was talking about. Didn't you know that when a woman is sexually aroused, her pupils dilate? And yours are telling me loud and clear all I need to know, Robin."

Before she could protest his arrogance, his arms had pulled her close, his fingers tangling in her hair and holding her fast, his mouth seeking the warmth of hers. It had been a few weeks since he had kissed her, and the unexpected flames of pleasure that his touch evoked in her numbed her for a few exquisite moments. She was unable to resist, totally and wantonly under his spell, responding without wanting to.

Somewhere in her conscious mind a warning voice whispered to her to stop this right now, to remember that Luke was the enemy. But she smothered the voice, lost in sensation, dizzy with desire. He awoke every dormant need in her.

She could feel the drum of Luke's heartbeats, as rapid as her own. Somehow he managed to hold her close, despite the awkwardness of their position. She wouldn't let herself think that he was so practised in this. . . . She didn't want to think at all, only to feel.

"Luke," she breathed faintly, when he finally ended the kiss, only to touch her mouth over and over with his lips in tiny ghost kisses.

"Now tell me you feel nothing for me." His arrogant, relentless voice seemed to echo in her head. "I don't believe you can lie to yourself, Robin, so don't lie to me!"

"I never pretended to feel *nothing* for you." These double negatives were confusing her as much as his nearness. She didn't know what she felt anymore. *Love, hate, aggression*—all those words were applicable in some measure. Luke's palm softly caressed her breast. She heard him draw in his breath a little at her hardened nipples. They spoke, too, saying what she refused to admit in words: that Luke was the most exciting man she had ever known. The one she wanted.

And he wanted her. *Wanted* . . . not loved, as he had no doubt *wanted* so many other women—not loved. And Robin needed to be loved if she was to surrender herself, her body and soul, to a man. To share herself with anyone—that total commitment—demanded no less in return. And nothing less than love would do. The receptionist's cheerful words soared into her mind.

"Love 'em and leave 'em, that's what Luke does."

And Robin knew she couldn't bear it if she ended up as one of his castoffs. Appalled at the way her thoughts were going, she checked them right there and pushed him away from her with an angry gesture.

"All right, you've had your fun," she mumbled, praying he wouldn't know what an effort it cost her to behave that way. "It's all a game to you, isn't it, Luke?"

She saw the set look on his craggy features and knew she had angered him by her snub. His blue eyes spat fire at her and the muscles in his jaw were tightly stretched, the cords in his neck standing out. For a moment he looked as if he wanted to take her in his arms and shake her, and she visibly shrank back in her seat.

His mouth twisted sardonically as he spoke. "Don't worry, I'm not going to molest you again, Robin. And just what little game are you playing? I wonder. You wanted me just now as much as I want you. Is this your usual style, leading a man on and then giving him the big freeze?"

Hot tears threatened to spill over, and she blinked them back furiously.

"I did not lead you on! I asked you a perfectly innocent question, which you still haven't answered. I didn't expect you to leap on me like an—an animal."

"Forgive me." He oozed sarcasm. "I thought you said you weren't a fragile plant. What was the question, anyway? I seem to have forgotten it."

"I asked why you'd been so distant lately," she said coldly. "It just seemed out of character—and I've been proved right, haven't I? Is this the way you operate, confusing your victims until they wonder what they're supposed to have done to upset you?"

He paused. "Is that what you thought?" he said at last. He moved fractionally away from her, and to Robin's surprise he looked almost embarrassed; at least, in any other man she would have called it embarrassment. Luke hid his feelings well, and she couldn't be sure.

"If you must know, I had a good talking-to about you!"

Robin gaped at him. Not her father, surely. Her face burned. Oh, he couldn't have. She was a grown woman, capable of running her own life. She couldn't believe James would have done such a thing. Luke's next words dispelled the thought.

"My dear housekeeper decided you were too nice a girl to be caught in my clutches, as she so eloquently put it," he said coolly. "Mrs. Somerton apparently got the idea that your tearful face on the night you arrived in town was due to my advances—as if you weren't able to put down any man who came within a mile of you, as I assured her. But since she's known me since childhood, she decided to lecture me on how rotten I was being, taking you away from home and then trying to seduce you. She made me feel like the big bad wolf, so to please her I decided to keep my distance. Satisfied?"

While he was talking, several things dawned on Robin. Firstly, he respected Mrs. Somerton and paid attention to what she said, whether mistaken or not. Secondly, despite the laconic way he spoke and the attempt to be amusing, there was a distinct note of anxiety in his voice, almost as if he had seriously been reflecting on the housekeeper's words, reviewing their own situation and perhaps having second thoughts about the wisdom of upsetting James Pollard's daughter, whether because James might cancel the deal—that is, if he was allowed to under the terms of their contract—or because he felt slightly guilty about trying to seduce his own business partner's daughter.

One thing Robin was quite sure about: She had no intention of asking Luke the true reason! Instead she took his words at their face value, giving a brief nod.

"Thank you for telling me. I'd prefer it if we kept our association on a business level from now on." She could be as cold as ice when she chose.

Luke switched on the car engine, preparatory to descending the steep, narrow country road to inspect the building site below.

"During working hours, certainly," he retorted. "After that, I'd say it's every man for himself."

"You have a talent for putting things crudely," Robin said freezingly.

"That's just where you're wrong," Luke said as the car roared off at far too fast a speed, proving how nettled he really was. "There's nothing crude about a man desiring a lovely woman. It's what life is all about, Robin, and if you're too shortsighted to see that, then I'm sorry for you. We could have had a marvellous relationship, but if you don't want to know . . ."

He left it unsaid, but the silence said it all. If Robin didn't want him, there'd be no shortage of women who did. And she never doubted it. For the rest of the day, while she tried to take in the information the site manager was telling her and Luke, and during the long drive back to her flat, Robin was tight with tension, wondering just what she was throwing away. And what was more, wondering *why*.

It was too late for them to go back to the office that afternoon. Luke had driven unsmilingly for the last ten miles, and Robin was conscious of suppressed misery. Even when they were battling verbally, there was some contact between them. This silence seemed to stretch interminably like some endless void, and she felt empty and depressed.

She needed food, she thought feverishly. She had some steak in her fridge. She'd cook herself a meal of steak and french fries and pretend she was at the Ritz. But she knew it wasn't lack of food that was turning her stomach upside down. As the car jerked to a stop, she started to get out with a feeling of utter relief. She couldn't take much more of this silent hostility. Luke's voice made her jump.

"I propose going down to Cornwall next week to see how the work's progressing. I shall stay several days. Do you want to come with me? Maureen's used to holding the fort here for short periods of time."

The smile was spreading across her face before he finished speaking. She felt like hugging him, only she didn't. But she couldn't disguise the warmth in her voice.

"Oh, Luke, yes! It will be lovely to see my father again, and the weather will still be good down there." She hesitated, but it would be just too churlish to expect him to stay in a hotel this time. "You'll stay at the manor with us, of course. Dad will expect me to ask you, I'm sure."

"Since you put it so graciously, I accept." Luke was smiling too, if rather stiffly, and Robin breathed more easily. It would be simply impossible to work together if they were not on speaking terms, and her father would sense the animosity immediately. At least while they were in Cornwall they had better give the appearance of being on good terms, or James would only worry about her. Adult or not, she was still his one ewe-lamb, as he used to tell her.

"Thank you, Luke," she said quietly.

"What for? It's business, remember? I need to inspect the site. I never leave a site without personal inspection and involvement for too long. My reputation is at stake."

She smiled again. His eyes were telling a story as well now, and she realized it was the best way he knew of smoothing things between them. He didn't have to ask her along. She pressed her hand on his arm for a moment.

"Thanks anyway," she said, and got out of the car.

She felt wilted once she reached her flat, turning on the radio for instant company. Luke had drained her. She was at once stimulated by him and antagonised by him. She tried to understand her feelings for him. If the little matter of the holiday complex above her beloved private cove didn't get in the way, she knew she would think about him entirely differently, finding in him the Romeo to her Juliet, the Tristram to her Isolde.

She passed a trembling hand across her forehead. Those fictional characters were all lovers, soul mates, partners in love. Robin thought she had gleaned enough about Luke Burgess by now to know that love didn't come into his involvements—not the kind of love that lasted a lifetime, the kind Robin yearned for. If it did . . . if she once believed that Luke really cared for her, enough to make a lasting commitment, how would she feel? How *did* she feel?

She wouldn't even let herself surmise the answer to that one. It was so unlikely that it wasn't worth her thinking time. She wouldn't let herself fantasise for one single moment how it would be to be truly loved by Luke, loved and wanted for all time.

"Don't be a fool," she told herself aloud, her voice shaking. "Get a hold of yourself and remember the vital issue. It's only Dad's land he wants, and you're just an added bonus."

But she knew now that he didn't go in for double-dealing in business, so it rather cut the ground from under her arguments. She smiled wryly as the pun struck her, then angrily tried to push Luke out of her mind as she went into the kitchen to prepare her meal. The fact still remained that the holiday complex was going to ruin the serenity of the Cornish scene, she thought caustically, and no amount of sweet talk or anything else was going to change her feelings about that!

Once she had eaten, she felt more relaxed and decided to phone her father to tell him of her forthcoming visit. She could hear the delight in his voice as he replied.

"That's wonderful, darling, and you sound so much better now. Not working you too hard, is he?"

"Oh, no! Quite the contrary. I'm enjoying the work, as a matter of fact." To her surprise she knew she spoke the truth. The job was interesting and always changing, and if it weren't for Luke's occasional disturbing assaults on her senses, she'd be enjoying it even more.

"Good. It's a change from your last job, but sometimes it's good to break away completely and do something new. When do you plan to come down, Robin?"

"I'm not sure which day yet. Luke just said next week, so I'll have to phone you again and let you know. And, Dad, I've asked him to stay at the manor this time. It's all right, isn't it? I felt I could hardly do anything else."

"Of course it is, darling. I like the man, and after all, he is my partner in a way. You'll both be very welcome."

She remembered his last words when she'd hung up. They seemed to unite her and Luke more as a married couple than as business acquaintances. Robin was losing patience with herself and the way her thoughts kept straying to no-go areas. She looked out of the window. It was a mellow night, softly dark, and she felt restless. Impulsively she changed into a sweater, slacks and jacket, and spent an exhilarating hour tramping over the Downs. The sounds of city traffic were muted up here, and if she let herself dream just a little, she could almost imagine she was striding over the moors at home, over bracken and heather, with the scent of gorse and wildflowers to tease her nostrils.

She hadn't been so nostalgic for a long time. While she had worked for Elaine Fowler her job had taken up all her thinking time, and Cornwall had always been there to go back to. It still was, but now Mrs. Fowler was gone, Robin knew herself to be more vulnerable than she had ever been. It was one more reason why it was so dangerous to let herself dream of things that could never be.

She was on her way home now, and the evening was getting chilly. Robin was almost alongside Luke's house, and she could see the lighted downstairs window of the lounge. She couldn't resist picturing him inside, maybe sitting in an easy chair and listening to music or reading . . . or maybe right now he was in there smiling into some woman's face and giving her all the benefit of his charm over Mrs. Somerton's superb cooking.

The image faded abruptly. Robin didn't want to imagine any more. She strode on to her own building, pulled the curtains firmly across the windows and sat in front of the television, hardly noticing the flickering pictures on the screen and hoping that the thing she dreaded most wasn't really happening to her. Falling in love with Luke would be so easy, as effortless as breathing, and it was the one thing she was determined not to do. Her soft, sensitive mouth took on a mutinous line.

He was invading her territory and spoiling the entire landscape. She had to keep that thought uppermost. She had been against the whole project from the minute her father had told her about it. In Robin's eyes he had sold them out to Luke Burgess, and to let herself fall under the man's spell would be a betrayal of herself. She didn't want to consider whether it was more important to love a piece of land or the man; she could cherish the first for all time, whereas Luke's loves were reputedly things of the moment.

Even Mrs. Somerton had said almost as much, to quote Luke's own words!

"*. . . too nice a girl to be caught in my clutches . . .*"

Didn't that say it all? If his devoted housekeeper

thought him a womaniser, then Robin would be foolish to allow herself to love him. She shivered suddenly, switched off the television programme she had hardly seen and went to bed. She wouldn't think about him one more minute. Instead she'd think about the visit to her home.

Chapter Seven

They drove down to Cornwall the following Tuesday and planned to be back on Friday, since Luke had a pressing meeting that afternoon. Robin didn't have to be there, and she toyed with the idea of staying on for the weekend and taking the train back to Bristol, but finally decided against it. Sunday trains were notoriously slow, and besides, she was enjoying her new surroundings in Bristol. She realised it with a little start of surprise.

James welcomed her with open arms. If there was a little awkwardness in their arrival, she put it down to Luke's reticence while she embraced her father. Mrs. Drew showed him to his room, which gave James and Robin a little time to themselves.

"How's it going?" James asked her. "Do you like the work?"

Robin smiled. "You mean are we at each other's throats yet, don't you? Not all the time! It's interesting enough work, Dad, and—" She paused.

"And?" James prompted. "You've discovered your father's not quite the idiot you took him for, I hope. Luke's no charlatan, is he?"

"No," she admitted. "All right, you win there. It doesn't change anything, though, does it? My cove will never be the same again, and the tourists will have eroded away another little bit of Cornwall."

The resentment was still there. For a while she had been able to ignore it. Away from there the prospect wasn't so appalling. Now, there, everything was suddenly larger than life again. Luke came into the room while they were still discussing it, and she couldn't help glaring at him. Why not? It was all his fault, after all. If he hadn't come down there, surveying the land and seeing her cove as a little gold mine, the tranquility of the place would still be undisturbed. And she would never have met Luke Burgess and been thrown into turmoil because of him. She couldn't keep the thought from rippling through her mind.

"Have you seen how the work's progressing, James?" Luke spoke to him directly, but Robin knew full well he was aware of her hostility. She could sense it in his voice and by the tightening of his jaw.

"I'm staggered at the speed of it all," James said with admiration. "You certainly move fast, Luke."

This time Robin avoided looking at him. There were two ways of agreeing to that, she thought savagely.

"It's no problem." Luke shrugged. "Pay the men enough and they'll put in the hours. When I see a good proposition, I see no point in wasting time."

Were all his words calculated to convey a double meaning, Robin wondered, or was she being extra sensitive? They had arrived in time for lunch, and she heard Luke say that as soon as they had eaten, he'd like to get down and inspect the site.

"I'll come with you both," James said, and Robin

knew he was as eager for the success of the project as Luke. She felt betrayed all over again, yet she couldn't deny that it had given her father a much-needed interest. His reluctant role as country squire bored him. He looked fit and well, and confided that he visited the site most days as an agreeable exercise.

"Good," Luke said. "It's as well to let the workmen see you there often."

To keep an eye on them, Robin thought immediately. She looked at him with open dislike, glad to have something positive to complain about.

"That's a bit snide, isn't it? Do you always like to have someone snooping about to crack the whip for your pound of flesh?"

"Robin!" Her father was outraged. "I think that remark was entirely unnecessary!"

Luke smiled in amusement, which enraged her more.

"It's all right, James, your daughter and I often strike sparks off each other. I'd let this one pass, since I'm enjoying your hospitality, but out of respect to you and in my own defence, I must make Robin understand that it's not like that at all. I have first-class managers on every site, and the workmen do an excellent job, but it's my belief that everybody likes a bit of encouragement now and then. To see one of the bosses taking an obvious interest in progress is a great advantage, so I thank you for it, James."

He managed to demoralise her so smoothly, showing her to be ungracious and bitchy. She hated him for doing that to her, even more because his words sounded so convincing and she didn't want to think the best of him. It was so much easier on her to think the worst. But for her father's sake she muttered an apology. This visit was going to be fraught with tension if she jumped on every little thing he said.

After lunch they all pulled on anoraks and heavy boots. The seasons were changing, and although Cornwall's climate was mellower than that of the rest of the country, nights were chilly and sometimes damp, and the ground had a decidedly sticky quality to it. Robin realised it could be dangerous work, gouging out an entire hillside for a holiday complex. Naturally a little thing like that wouldn't stop Luke Burgess.

When they reached the hillside above the cove, a biting wind brought the glowing colour to their faces. Far below, the sea was a threshing grey beneath a cloudy sky, very different from the idyllic blue of summer. But it wasn't the sea that caught Robin's attention. She had seen it too often, in all its moods. She gasped at the sight that met her eyes.

The whole hillside was desecrated, in her opinion. Great earth-moving machines droned and grated, spewing out huge mounds of the rich red earth with the ease of butter scoops. Already the hillside was stepped to accommodate the villas, and the former soft greenery was gone, leaving it sad and bare . . . bare, except for the teams of men working away in heavy outdoor clothes and yellow safety hats Robin recognised, imprinted with BURGESS DEVELOPMENTS around the rims.

The whole place throbbed with activity, and she swallowed back the lump in her throat, wishing she'd never come. To see it like this . . . Luke clasped her hand, holding it so tightly that she was unable to pull it away as she wanted to.

"Don't be upset, Robin." He was gentle, making the tears prick her eyelids even more, because she wanted to hate him, not let herself be swayed by soft words. "You've seen all the plans and the mock-ups. You know what the final look of it will be."

"Oh, yes, I'd forgotten," she said bitterly. "Instant trees, wasn't it? To hide the fact that strangers lurk behind every one of them, spoiling everything!"

She knew she was being unreasonable, childish, all the things he had ever accused her of, but she couldn't help it. Perhaps if she'd never seen the actual preparations, the destruction of something that had been so beautiful the last time she saw it would not be affecting her so. She wished she'd stayed at the office, but how could she have done that, with the chance to see her father for a few days so tempting?

James couldn't hear their exchange of words at that moment. He was already making his way carefully to where the site manager was coming to greet him, a smile of welcome on his face. There was clearly no antagonism there, Robin thought grudgingly. Luke suddenly spoke very close to her cheek.

"You're the one who's spoiling it for your father, Robin. Can't you see that? The project has given him a new interest, and having a sulking daughter around him isn't going to endear you to him."

"Thanks for the pep talk. When I need a shrink I'll come to you for advice," she said sarcastically.

The infuriating thing was that he spoke the truth. James was truly absorbed by all that was going on, and clearly didn't quite understand her continued animosity towards Luke. She heard him give an expressive oath, then yank at her hand.

"Come on. Show a little interest at least," he snapped. "If I were your father, I'd put you across my knee and spank you!"

"If you were my father, I'd leave home!"

"I was under the impression you'd already done that a long time ago. Forgive me for getting you all wrong. I hadn't realised you were still such a child. The grown-up packaging must have given a lot of men the wrong idea. Do you always run home to Daddy when one of them makes a pass at you?"

She couldn't scream abuse at him the way she wanted to because they had caught up with her father and the site manager by now, and she had to stand and burn inside while she made polite conversation and asked intelligent questions. She saw all too well the pleasure her father took from her apparent approval of all that was going on. For his sake only, she vowed to herself, she would allow the dust to settle.

Inside she still seethed, more bruised by Luke's scathing words than she would admit—and forced to think about them. Was she, after all, behaving in an entirely irrational and immature way, burying her head in the sand completely on a childish whim? She had always considered herself to be fairly sophisticated and mature until now—until she met Luke Burgess. No one else had ever spoken to her the way he did, or irritated her so much. Or filled her mind to the exclusion of all else.

She followed the men back to the top of the hill, ignoring anyone's helping hand, pausing with them to catch her breath. When the complex was complete, there would be a winding road to the villas. Right now it seemed impossible to visualise it. All she could see were vast quantities of mud.

"Well, Robin?" James asked her eagerly, as pleased as if he'd moved every mound of earth himself. "Aren't you amazed at how quickly it's all progressing?"

At least she could answer that honestly.

"Absolutely," she said. "I guess money can buy nearly anything after all. I mean, in terms of work force, of course. Not everybody can get workmen agreeing to a seven-day week. I've got to hand it to you, Luke."

She knew all about the work force, since she dealt with the pay slips in the office. She knew how generous Luke was with his bonuses. And she knew her little barb about money being able to buy nearly everything hadn't gone unnoticed. What she was really saying was that it couldn't buy *her*.

"Let's get back to the house," James said. "I find the climb back up a bit strenuous these days. A reviving cup of tea is what I need now."

Robin looked at him anxiously. All their faces were flushed from the wind and the exertion of the climb, but while it had made little difference to her and Luke, James was still breathing heavily. He brushed aside her quick concern with a teasing comment that he thought he'd last out the day.

"Don't overdo it, Dad. After all, it's not your problem if the men are slackening, is it? And from the looks of them, I'd say it was unlikely."

"Robin thinks I'm a slave driver." Luke had caught her meaning at once, as she had meant him to, and James glanced from one to the other of them in mild exasperation.

"Do you two always go on like this? It must make for entertainment in the office among the rest of the staff!"

Robin gave a short laugh. "Luke's not in the office very much." Which was just as well. She didn't finish the sentence, but the implication was there, and her father gave a little sigh. He had the Cornishman's romantic streak under that gruff exterior, Robin remembered with a rush of affection and wry humour. By now he was probably imagining herself and Luke in the midst of a romantic involvement, considering himself a bit of a matchmaker in inadvertently throwing them together. He couldn't be more wrong, she thought, with an unwilling, heart-catching wrench.

If she had met and known Luke Burgess under any

other circumstances—if he were any other man but the one who was tearing the heart and soul out of her corner of the world—then she could have fallen so tempestuously in love with him. . . . She blocked off the thought at once, refusing to give it houseroom.

Luke had said there was no need for her to stay close to him on the second day they were in Cornwall. He wanted to spend much of the day at the site, taking his manager out to lunch at a pub and discussing the finer details with him in a friendly atmosphere. She couldn't help admiring his understanding of human nature. No wonder his colleagues rallied round him one hundred percent. He expected the best and he got it. She had to give him that much.

So it was something of a relief the next morning to spend some time with her father, lazing about and talking over old times and her new life as Luke's secretary. It was only a temporary arrangement, she insisted to him. She had no intention of being Luke's slave forever!

James laughed. "You either have a real hang-up about the man or you're in love with him, my darling daughter!"

"And you've been watching too many Western films on TV again," she answered smartly. "A real hang-up indeed!"

He didn't comment on how neatly she had avoided the issue. "So what will you do when this temporary arrangement has ended? And just how temporary is it going to be?" he went on relentlessly.

Robin shrugged her slim shoulders. "Until I see this job through, I suppose." Her voice was grim. "That's what I intended in the first place."

"To check up on whether he was fiddling a dim-witted old man, wasn't it?" He spoke with his tongue in his cheek and saw her blush.

"All right, so I was wrong about that. I'm willing to

admit it! It doesn't alter anything, though, does it, Dad? I simply can't see a modern holiday complex blending in with the quiet of the country down here. It doesn't fit. And stop calling yourself dim-witted. You're a match for anyone, including me, and you know it."

"Especially you, I'd say," he said mildly. "I think I know you better than you know yourself, my love, and methinks the lady does protest too much."

"Let's change this conversation, shall we? I see enough of Luke Burgess without wanting to discuss him all the time, and I came to see you, remember?" But she couldn't resist one more thing: "From what I've seen of the site, I know I was right, and you'll see it, too, eventually. You can't bring a futuristic complex to Cornwall. It's a violation of all its history, and I'm not going to say another word on the subject!"

She clamped her lips together with firm determination, and James wisely said no more. Instead they discussed mutual acquaintances and light topics, and if he noticed how often her eyes strayed to the carriage clock on the mantel, he didn't comment on it. Robin was angry at herself for picturing Luke's movements that afternoon, seeing him through lunch and poring over the site plans with his manager, then going back to the hillside, charming even the most rugged workmen with his own enthusiasm for the project. She shivered a little, finally saying she would have a bath before dinner and leaving her father to his own reflections.

She had a long, leisurely soak in scented water, letting the perfumed bubbles caress her smooth, golden skin. Her father had stirred up thoughts about the future and what she intended to do once she left Luke's employ.

A pang shot through her, for she had no idea at all. She hadn't thought beyond the months in which the complex was being built, seeing herself as a kind of crusader; the thought seemed utterly foolish now. What was she accomplishing, anyway? Working for Luke seemed futile and was changing nothing. If anything, it gave Luke an excuse to crow over her, for as well as having her father his so-called partner, he had the other member of the Pollard family dependent on him while she was in his employ.

She should have seen that in the beginning. She was becoming angry with herself. And when the job was finished she would have to start looking around for something else, because there was no way she would continue to be beholden to him. She would miss him, of course. She couldn't stop the thought rushing into her mind. He had become part of her life. He had stormed into it and turned it upside down.

Robin quickly let out the bathwater, not wanting those images to intrude any longer. They were too disturbing, too sensual, too much like an adolescent's fantasies—too all-consuming. She dried herself with a huge fluffy bath towel, then wrapped a bathrobe around her slender body and cooled off in her bedroom before dinner.

She would stay up there, relaxing, making her mind a void for half an hour before meeting Luke for the next verbal onslaught. That was her last waking thought, a rueful smile curving her soft, expressive mouth before she drifted into a light sleep.

When she awoke, having long ago schooled herself to doze for just the right length of time, Robin felt refreshed and alert. She dressed for dinner in a soft peach-coloured dress that her father particularly liked and wore an emerald necklace that had belonged to her mother. It was a stunning foil for her eyes, and though a little dated for her taste, it pleased James when she wore it. And naturally it was all for his benefit.

All the same, she was feminine enough to feel a glow of pleasure at the way Luke's eyes widened a little as she came downstairs. Luke came to meet her and she guessed at once that he must have showered or bathed too. Gone were the casual clothes; instead he wore a light-blue jacket and slacks and a shirt and tie. His dark hair was still a little damp, curling slightly against his nape and sending out a faint scent of pine, earthy and sensual. Knowing that James liked to dress for dinner at the manor, Robin felt absurdly pleased that Luke had remembered and taken the trouble.

He moved towards the bottom of the stairs as she came down. "You look beautiful," he said softly. "But then, you always do."

The compliment was so simple, so natural, that she hardly knew what to say. He held out his hand to her, and when she put her own in his strong, firm grasp, she felt his fingers curl around hers, warmly possessive. She had to fumble for words.

"Thank you, Luke." She hesitated. "And just for tonight, can we be friends?"

His grip tightened. "For always, I hope, whatever else we are."

She let the enigmatic comment pass. She wanted the evening to progress amicably, without the unbearable tension that inevitably grew between her and Luke. James already knew it existed, but Robin wanted to spare him this last evening.

James would only fret about her if he thought she was unhappy in Luke's employ. The thought struck her oddly, because so far, happiness or unhappiness hadn't really entered their relationship. She could apply plenty of other words—*tension, passion, anger, suspicion,* even *lust,* she thought, certainly on his side—but nothing more. And that was enough!

"Robin, my dear, you look lovely." Her father's

voice interrupted her thoughts, and Luke released her hand as she went forward to kiss James's cheek, seeing his gaze on the emerald necklace.

"Thanks, Dad." She received the compliment from him far more easily and brought things down to a less emotional level by saying she was famished and that all that Cornish air was giving her an enormous appetite.

"You're not used to it, darling." James smiled at her. "You've lived in London for too long, and now you're in Bristol. You may not know it, but you're becoming more of a city girl than a country one!"

His words gave her a little shock. She denied them at once. "How can you say such a thing? Cornwall is my home, where my roots are."

"But is it where your heart is?" James said quizzically.

"Well, of course it is. The two go together, don't they?" She didn't look at Luke, but from the corner of her eye she could see him watching her, a half-smile playing around his mouth at her defence of her home county.

As they went in to dinner she still felt a little disturbed by his comment. How could she be called a city girl! She loved Cornwall too much. Even as she thought it, Robin realised that for the past years, while she had been in Elaine Fowler's employ, Cornwall had been no more than a well-loved, familiar place to come back to for short spells.

Had she been so vulnerable after the shock of Mrs. Fowler's death that she had clung to Cornwall as a refuge while her mind healed, much as a child clings to a security blanket? And if Luke hadn't been the catalyst that stirred her into defence of her home county, would she have come out of her depression so quickly? Maybe she owed him something after all. At least raw anger was preferable to plunging despair and the numbness she'd felt after finding her employer dead.

"I can't blame Robin for feeling distressed in the first place when she heard about the development, James," Luke was saying smoothly, just as if he could guess at her whirling thoughts. "The conservationists have a wonderful champion in her."

"It's a bit late to be saying that now, isn't it?" The words were out before she could stop them, forgetting her decision to keep this evening calm and placid. Her eyes flashed at him across the table, a fire that matched that of the jewels around her neck.

"I was discussing the complex with your father before you came down, Robin," he went on coolly, as if to prove that he wasn't the one who had provoked the animosity.

"And you're going to put all the earth back and replant the turf, are you?" she said sarcastically, knowing it was as unlikely as flying to the stars, though man was fast succeeding in even that impossible task now, she thought uneasily. And Luke would probably try that if he thought there was land to be developed.

He laughed, refusing to be goaded. "Hardly! No, what I think you need is to see one of my successful complexes, identical to the one we're building here, to prove once and for all how well it blends in with the existing scenery. I'm not trying to disrupt the whole way of life here, nor am I playing God and thinking I can change the face of the earth."

"Really?" she asked innocently, letting her eyes widen, and had the satisfaction of seeing his jawline tighten a little. Despite his efforts at keeping calm for her father's sake and for the sake of good manners, she knew she was getting to him.

And almost at once she bit her lip a little. She had been the one to suggest that they act as friends—for the evening, at least—and she knew she was being bitchy instead.

"I'm sorry, Luke. Please go on," she said hurriedly. "What do you have in mind?"

"Just what I said. I think you should see another complex before you condemn me completely." His voice was terse, as if he'd had enough of the conversation.

"Well, that's all right by me. How can I object? You're the boss, after all. If you want to take me along to look at a row of buildings, then okay." The statement was meant to be agreeable, but it came out as anything but that.

She was half surprised that her father hadn't made any comments of his own, but glancing at him, Robin could see he was actually enjoying this little battle of words. She had always let her tongue run away with her. It was one of her failings, and she guessed that James was enjoying the fact that at last she had met her match. Luke wasn't the type of man to let her get away with anything.

Men she had known in the past had fallen by the wayside, either because her sometimes caustic tongue had put them off, despite her vivacious personality and physical loveliness, or because they simply hadn't been male enough for her, with the strong characteristics her own nature demanded. They simply hadn't measured up. There was no doubt that Luke Burgess was a man in every sense of the word. She saw him smile at her put-down of his work, as if it mattered little to him what she thought, which in itself should have made her suspicious.

"It's agreed, then. We'll go early next week. I've a few pressing matters to attend to in Bristol before then, but Monday should be all right." He was businesslike and brusque.

"Fine," Robin said distantly, the secretary agreeing

to the Great One's wishes without demur. "Am I allowed to ask where this other complex is situated?"

"No, you're not." He smiled again. "I don't want you to form any ideas until we get there. We'll stay a couple of days, though, and you can discover firsthand what the accommodations are like from the tourists' viewpoint."

She was about to say that she didn't think that was a good idea at all, when his next words stopped her.

"Oh, and you'd better pack a few lightweight clothes, including a swimsuit, or that delicious bikini I first saw you wearing. And don't forget your passport."

Chapter Eight

It was easy to see that James thought it a marvellous idea. He could see nothing wrong in Luke, Robin thought, to her amazement. And no matter how hard she tried to pin Luke down to telling her where they were going, Luke refused, saying that he didn't want her to have any biased thoughts before they arrived—saying, too, that she needn't go back to the office before they set off on Monday morning.

He was brisk and businesslike, and if she had suspicions about his motives, she decided to ignore them. She was determined to see the complex he referred to and know just how spoiled her own patch of earth was going to be. It was devastated already, as far as she was concerned, but maybe seeing the holiday complex that was already flourishing would prove to her finally that Luke had no soul and that all he was interested in was the pound in his pocket.

He called for her around ten-thirty on Monday

morning and put her small suitcase alongside his in the back of the car. Trickles of alarm ran through her, just seeing the two suitcases together, but it was too late to back out now, ridiculous to even think of it. She wasn't so feeble that she couldn't hold off his amorous advances, if that was what he had in mind.

"Which airline are we flying with?" she asked casually, with a fleeting hope that she might glean some idea of their destination. Luke merely smiled.

"We're flying from Lulsgate. Don't worry, if you suffer from airsickness, there are some pills in the car."

"I don't," she snapped. "I'm just getting tired of all this cloak-and-dagger stuff. You're not abducting me, by any chance?"

Luke laughed, a rich, warm sound that made the blood flow faster in her veins. "It's an attractive idea, but I've no wish to sell you off in some Arab slave market, and I think my partnership with your father would be badly strained if I didn't bring you safely back to England."

And didn't that just confirm that business was more important to him than anything else! Robin's mouth tightened, not sure whether to be relieved or annoyed.

"We're not going to be away very long, then?" Her tone said that too many days alone with him would be odious, and the smile curving his mouth faded.

"Just one night, I think," he said curtly. "I'll get you back in time to watch your favourite TV programme tomorrow night. I got you all wrong, Robin. That first day I saw you at the beach I took you for a real outdoor girl, with a fascinating touch of sophistication. Certainly not the sort of girl who would prefer to curl up with the television instead of a real-life man. . . ."

"At least you know where you are with TV men," she whipped back. "You can turn them off with the flick of a switch."

"Oh, there are other ways of turning a man off, darling," he said coolly, putting a different meaning on the words, and she felt her face flame with colour. Well, so what? She hadn't asked for any involvement with him apart from a business one, and although she intended sticking it out until the Cornish holiday complex was complete, just to keep her eye on things, Robin knew it would be less of a strain on her emotions once she was well away from him.

She didn't rise to his taunt and sat in silence as the car covered the relatively short distance to Lulsgate and the airport that served Bristol and the district. He couldn't keep it from her now, Robin thought. Once she saw the desk in the departure lounge, she'd know where they were heading.

"Let me have your passport to hurry up the formalities," Luke said once they had parked the car and were nearing the building. She handed it over. It made no difference. He couldn't keep it secret much longer, and privately she thought it was a silly game he was playing to try to do so.

The airport was full of people taking late holidays in the sun, and Robin had to keep her eyes on Luke's tall figure as he moved purposefully through them. She experienced a little shock as she realised he wasn't making for any of the airline desks. Minutes later, the formalities completed, she was walking beside him to a small private plane that was waiting on the tarmac, away from the main airline runways.

Robin's heart jolted. She didn't mind flying, but she had always flown in big jets, smoothly and comfortably. She felt her mouth go dry as several airport employees appeared to tell Luke that the plane was fuelled and cleared for takeoff as soon as he was at the controls.

It was a bit like dreamland, Robin thought faintly. She hadn't bargained on this, but she'd die rather than let him see how nervous she was or how bizarre she was finding the whole situation. What was she doing there? And yet, what was more logical, under normal circumstances, than a boss taking his secretary on a brief business trip? As long as it stayed strictly business.

"Surprised?" Luke asked as he held her elbow while she mounted the steps to the plane. She managed a nonchalant shrug.

"Nothing about you surprises me, Luke," she replied scathingly, knowing it to be a gross understatement.

"Really?" He grinned. "I'll have to try harder, then, won't I? I'd hate for our relationship to become boring."

"We don't have a relationship," she said, sitting in the seat he pointed to, praying he wouldn't notice how her hands shook as she fastened the seat belt or guess at the butterflies in her stomach.

"Oh, yes we do," he said aggressively as he took up his position in the pilot's seat. "Whether it's the one either of us wants, Robin, is something else again. But you can't deny that there's a chemical reaction between us."

"Just as there is one between oil and water, and you know what happens there," she retorted.

"I hope you and I are not destined to repel each other that way. It's certainly not the way I feel about you."

She couldn't tell whether he was being sincere or fatuous. She didn't want to think about it at that moment. All she cared to think about was the fact that the engine was revving up. Her nails were digging little half-moons in her palms as she heard Luke switch on the airport-monitoring system, give concise details as to his course and receive the okay for takeoff. The destination wasn't mentioned, and Robin could only be thankful that she had no time to think about the fragility of the little plane before they were cruising along the tarmac and suddenly soaring skywards. It felt as if she had left her stomach somewhere in midair.

"It'll be all right once we level out," Luke's voice came back to her, kindly and half amused. "I did suggest taking a pill, Robin."

"I don't need one, thanks." She crossed her fingers as she spoke. "How long are we going to be up in this toy?"

"A couple of hours or so," he said, giving nothing away. "Relax and enjoy it—and stop pretending! You're as tense as a spring. This toy, as you call it, is as safe as an automobile. I've used it hundreds of times."

She tried to draw confidence from his words, and gradually some of the anxiety left her. They didn't fly as high as the jets, and that in itself was comforting. Robin could clearly make out the coastlines of England and France, and then the great mass of the latter country, its cities and mountains. Then Spain. She had come this way before, on a Spanish holiday. They were crossing water again, and by now she realised that she was so intrigued by the guessing game about their destination that she forgot to worry about the fragility of the small plane. She had to admit that Luke's handling of it was excellent.

Below them the sea glittered sapphire blue, with none of the pre-winter greyness of English seas. The terrain was a dusty brown, dotted with white buildings and greenery. The unmistakable name of the island suddenly appearing on the airport terminal as they came in to land made Robin catch her breath.

"Ibiza!"

"Have you been here before? Your father didn't think so."

So her father was in on the little conspiracy! Male chauvinism at its worst, Robin thought in annoyance, when Luke could involve her father in his little schemes. But she was too excited at the prospect of seeing the island to waste very much thinking time about it.

"No, I haven't, but I've always wanted to come. It's less spoiled than Majorca, isn't it?"

In her haste to cover her annoyance, Robin knew she had played right into Luke's hands as the plane circled to a stop and he turned to face her.

"So why do you think my complex is so acceptable here? The authorities don't let any old tin-pot firm in to spoil their island. I think you'll be agreeably surprised, and when you see my development, remember it's exactly the way the appalling building site you saw in Cornwall will look in a few months' time. Don't condemn me before then, Robin. Let's call a truce for now, all right?"

"All right," she said slowly. It seemed ungrateful to do otherwise, when he'd brought her there to that idyllic place, and she smothered her suspicions for the moment.

Stepping out into the sunlight was like suddenly finding an extension of summer. The air was pleasantly hot, without the baking heat of high season. The sky was cloudless, and a heat haze hung over the hills. Robin knew a stab of excitement. She was there, and she might as well enjoy it. She gave Luke the most unforced smile he'd received from her since their meeting.

"Thanks for the chance to come here, anyway, Luke."

"It's my pleasure," he said crisply, not letting her see how that smile affected him. Luke Burgess, who had had his share of women, was still quite unsure how this one had managed to make herself so special to him. He resorted to the old tricks.

"And if you feel like staying on after tomorrow, I'm sure it can be arranged."

He caressed her arm as they walked to the terminal, making no secret of his desire, and Robin knew she had only to say the word and this trip would turn into something very different from a mere business arrangement. She froze at once.

"I think you'll have had enough of me by tomorrow, Luke, because I've no intention of turning this into a holiday for lovers. If that's what you had in mind, forget it."

Her green eyes sparkled as she spoke, her golden hair caught the sunlight like fire and he pretended to back off in mock horror.

"Don't worry, I wouldn't get entangled in those spikes of yours for a king's ransom! There's no shortage of agreeable female company in Ibiza." He said it casually, as if it didn't matter to him that Robin was going to be standoffish. It was already clear to her that Luke was as well known there as in Bristol. He was greeted at the airport as an old friend, and again the formalities were minimal.

There was a rental car waiting for them, and Robin didn't miss the smiles directed at her from the officials with whom they came in contact. How many other girls had Luke brought to the island in his private plane, she thought instantly? And not for any business purpose, either. It was no concern of hers, as long as she wasn't classed with the rest of them.

"The complex isn't too far from here," Luke said

easily as they drove out of the airport and onto a wide main road. "We go through Ibiza town and then we head for one of the little bays along the coast. We're just to the north of one of the tourist spots, Cala Llonga."

The names meant nothing to Robin. It was only a short drive to Ibiza town. The old part of the town rose dramatically, topped by ancient walls and a church. In its colourful harbour were craft of every description. They drove slowly through the town, then on to narrower roads. The tang of the sea reminded Robin of home, but this was undeniably a Spanish island, with its white houses huddling against the hillsides and its dry, dusty atmosphere. Her spirit soared, and she felt the holiday mood catch her, despite everything.

They turned slightly inland for a while, and outside the town the island was a different place, almost deserted, as unspoiled as she had ever imagined it. She could smell the scent of pine on the crystal-clear air. It was the perfect get-away-from-it-all place, beautiful, dramatic.

The small resort of Cala Llonga was at the head of a long stretch of golden sand, as its name suggested. The road skirted the beach, and Robin could see plenty of lovely tanned bodies soaking up the sun. Someone like Luke would never need to be alone for long there, she thought cynically. She suddenly pictured him in swimming shorts, her imagination supplying the necessary details—wide bronzed chest matted with dark hair, lithe, athletic limbs, flat stomach . . .

Robin stopped her thoughts right there, wishing angrily that she had brought a one-piece swimsuit with her instead of the yellow bikini Luke had first seen her in. She had thrown it in the suitcase in a gesture of defiance, knowing that if she was going somewhere warm, she would be unable to resist the lure of the sea and sun. But she was damn well going to resist *him,* she thought bitingly.

They were driving along less than adequate roads then, and Luke turned to her with a grin as he slowed the car down.

"Away from the main roads, there are little more than dirt tracks in some places, so hold on to your seat," he warned her. "It gets rugged farther on."

She discovered that he spoke the truth. They seemed to be heading nowhere, through winding lanes that shook the car to its limits, sometimes steep, sometimes gently undulating, until at last the sea suddenly and gloriously came into full view once more. Luke brought the car to a stop and turned off the engine. The total silence took Robin's breath away for a moment.

"It's fantastic," she said at last. "You'd never know this little corner existed. I'm glad you showed it to me, Luke. How much farther do we have to go?"

"We're here," he said. She looked at him, startled, and then shielded her eyes against the sun as he pointed to the hillside next to them. It was so close that Robin hadn't even noticed it, but now she realised that nestling in amongst the trees were half a dozen cubelike white buildings with red Spanish-tile roofs, discreet and separated by screens of trees, in perfect harmony with their surroundings.

Luke was getting out of the car. When Robin followed him, he pointed down to a tiny strip of sand below the white complex.

"That's the exclusive beach belonging to the complex," he told her. "The agent who leases the villas for me makes it clear that access is limited, and the place is unlikely to appeal to people wanting the usual tourist amenities. No ice-cream vans get here and there are no beach shops or restaurants, just the villas and the beach. Does that answer all your questions?"

Robin was speechless for a moment. She hadn't expected anything like that. If she had ever thought that Luke was insensitive to the natural environment of a place, she had been wrong. Only someone with a very caring interest in the beauty of the island could have planned such a retreat. And she was honest enough to tell him so.

"I'm very impressed," she admitted. "And this is how the complex at home will look?"

"Give or take a certain quota of sun," he said. "I can't guarantee the English weather, but I can guarantee that I'm not the ogre you took me for. Give me credit for that, Robin!"

"I do," she said sincerely. "Can I take a look in one of the villas, or are they all occupied until the end of the season?" She didn't add that she couldn't imagine Luke letting any of them stay vacant. She mustn't let herself forget he was in this to make money, and from the look of those beautiful villas, it was no wonder he was successful.

"Naturally you can see inside," he said calmly. "This is where we're staying tonight."

Robin whirled to face him, the hot colour suddenly staining her face, hoping desperately he didn't mean it the way she thought he did. At the sardonic smile on his handsome face, she was left in little doubt.

"You—you—" she spluttered, her hands clenching at her sides. Luke caught hold of them, turning them palms-up and suddenly bending his lips to kiss each one.

The movement was so erotic, so unexpected, that it stopped Robin in her tracks for a moment—but only for a moment. She snatched her hands away and stepped back a pace.

"You're despicable, Luke," she snapped. "And if you think I'm staying there with you—"

"Where are you going, then? It's a couple of miles back to the main road, and eight miles back to Ibiza town if you're thinking of finding a hotel. It's a long walk, even with a small suitcase, but if that's what you want . . ."

He reached into the back seat and dumped her suitcase on the ground. She glared at him, furious at the way he'd trapped her. There was no way she could walk that far over the rough track, and there wasn't a single sign of anyone else in the villas or on the beach. He was beyond contempt for doing this to her.

"Are all the villas unoccupied?" she demanded, her green eyes flashing like fire. "Do you mean to say you've stopped lining your pockets for a few days in the hope that I'm going to spend the night with you here because I've no alternative? If that's the case, since there are six villas, I'll make darned sure we sleep in different ones!"

"That means you're staying, then." There was a glint of triumph in his eyes, to her fury. "And I'm sorry, darling, but five of them are occupied, and I think you're intelligent enough to know how many that leaves."

"I'm not staying in there with you," Robin said instantly.

She was brittle with tension, like a bird poised for flight when faced with a predator. It was exactly the way she thought of him. He had calculated all this, right down to making sure there was only one vacant villa. She was breathing heavily, and it was only her anger that was keeping her from bursting into tears. She hated him for his deception; she'd thought him above that. She hadn't thought even Luke would resort to such underhanded means.

"If you'll cool down a minute and just think, Robin,

you'll know there are two bedrooms in each villa. You've seen the plans and the layouts, so stop glaring at me like a little spitfire and get back in the car," he said shortly. "We can drive a bit farther yet. And just for the record, you'll be quite safe in your virginal bed tonight. There's no way I'd risk my neck with you after that little display of temper. I'd as soon try to seduce a shark. As I've said before, I can always find more congenial company."

She didn't answer for a minute, and the challenge in his eyes was almost primitive, male against female, aggressively asserting superiority. She would have dearly loved to march off into the sunset, but it would have been stupid and impractical. Her answer was to toss her suitcase back into the car and sit in the passenger seat, arms folded, a mutinous look in her eyes as she stared straight ahead.

Luke slid in beside her, saying nothing. He started up the car engine again and they moved slowly forward, around a few more bends in the lane, then gradually upwards towards the villas. Narrow tracks led to each one, tracks just wide enough to allow a car to approach and park alongside. From below, there had been no sign of any other cars, but Robin could just glimpse one in front of the next villa. He had spoken the truth, then, she thought grudgingly. There were other people there. The thought was both reassuring and annoying. She wasn't sure she would have fancied being one of the only two people in that quiet place, heavenly though it was. It might be a little eerie at night to be so entirely alone.

"I thought we'd called a truce," Luke said mildly as they stopped at the villa.

"That was before I knew you'd tricked me."

"But I didn't trick you." He oozed patience and self-confidence, and Robin could have hit him. "You knew where we were going, and if you couldn't have worked out for yourself that we'd be staying here, you're not very bright, Robin."

She was suddenly tired of all this fighting. "Luke, can we go inside, please? I'd like to see the view from up here."

"Of course. That's why we're here, after all. By the way, I thought we'd drive along the coast tonight for dinner. I know a wonderful seafood restaurant overlooking the ocean. I don't imagine you want to start cooking, do you?"

"Certainly not. I didn't come here to go all domestic." She especially didn't want a cozy dinner for two in a place so obviously made for lovers. His words relieved her a little. She intended spending as little time as possible actually inside the villa with him. He disturbed her too much. Not romantically right now, because she was still too incensed with him. It wasn't that she didn't trust herself to be alone with him, though she refused to let her thoughts dwell on the implications of that too much. She didn't trust *him*.

Luke carried the suitcases inside, and Robin freely admitted that the villa was beautiful. The furnishings were tasteful and elegant, yet still comfortable. There were two bedrooms, to her relief, each with a key in the lock. With no pretence at secrecy, Robin took out her key at once and slipped it into her bag. Luke noted the small action.

"There was no need. I told you, I shan't bother you. I don't normally seduce my secretaries."

He had put her in her place and at the same time made her feel less of a woman. She would have stamped her foot in fury if it hadn't been such a childish gesture. Instead she inspected the rest of the villa, including the immaculate kitchen. Its fridge was stocked with enough food for the time they were there; obviously Luke had ordered it in advance from the agent, whoever he was. And then there was the superb view from the picture window of the lounge, which opened out onto a small balcony with a white table and chairs for eating out-of-doors. The hazy blue ocean stretched invitingly far below, and now Robin could make out two figures walking along the private beach, arms entwined, oblivious to everything but each other.

She drew back, not because she was afraid of being seen, but because those two seemed to epitomise all that romantic Spanish island stood for: an island made for love, not for the intrusion of two people constantly bickering at each other, hating each other. . . . Her eyes suddenly prickled with tears, because she really didn't want it to be that way. Somehow she and Luke seemed destined to bring out the worst in each other.

She suddenly felt the touch of his hands on her waist. He stood behind her, and she could feel the steady beat of his heart as he pulled her against him. Her own was thudding too fast, too wildly, and his voice was feather-soft in her ear.

"You don't have to be afraid of me, Robin." He had obviously felt her tense. She wasn't sure if his voice was tender or mocking. "I've never forced myself on any woman. But if you change your mind about that locked door tonight, you only have to tap on the bedroom wall."

His hands had slid down to the curve of her hips, moving seductively in small spirals. For a few mindless seconds Robin's eyes closed as the wanton sensation his touch could arouse surged through her. There was no feeling of time passing, only the endless pleasure in submission to this man.

The intrusive sound of another voice brought Robin up sharply with a little shock. She must have been mad to let her guard slip for even an instant. It showed just how careful she must be. She was too vulnerable, and there in Ibiza it was all too easy for Luke to play on her emotions. She heard him mutter a small oath as he let her go, and then Robin realised that the voice she had heard was young and female and that it was floating towards them.

Chapter Nine

Robin turned at once, moving quickly away from Luke. The girl who had entered the villa, clearly very much at home there, wore only a brief bikini, and from the deep, glistening tán on every exposed bit of her body, Robin gucsscd she spent a great deal of her time at the beach. She was exotically beautiful, and she threw her arms around Luke's neck at once. It was a situation Robin could see he was enjoying.

"I thought I heard a car, Luke! Darling, it's so wonderful to see you again. I've missed you so much!" She spoke with a husky Spanish lilt, moulding herself voluptuously against Luke's body. If she noticed Robin at all, she chose to ignore her for the time being, giving all her attention to Luke.

He gave a laugh, extricating himself from her clinging arms—and doing so reluctantly, Robin thought. It just confirmed all she had ever surmised about him. Wherever he went, there would always be women like this one, welcoming him with their hot eyes and pouting lips.

"It's good to see you, too, Carlotta, and thanks for seeing to everything as usual. I want you to meet Robin. She's my secretary now, and the daughter of James Pollard. You've heard me mention him, haven't you? He owns the land on which I'm building the English complex identical to this one."

He must know this Carlotta extremely well, Robin thought, with a shaft of annoyance that her father's business had been discussed between them. She smiled a cool English smile at the stranger, and didn't miss the little gleam of speculation in Carlotta's eyes. She needn't worry! Robin hadn't come there as a rival to anyone, and Carlotta was welcome to him.

Luke spoke directly to Robin now. "Carlotta works as my agent in Ibiza," he said to her surprise. "She also sings at the casino during the summer and is the darling of the island. To unwind at the end of it all, she takes the last week of the tourist season in one of the villas here. That's some recommendation, isn't it?"

"I should think so," Robin murmured, not quite knowing what she was supposed to say. It was impossible to gauge the relationship between these two, but now she knew why Luke was so uncaring about her refusal to unlock her bedroom door to him. Why should he care, when he had all that Carlotta had to offer just a few doors away? Robin felt ridiculously deflated at the thought. Why couldn't the agent have been a man, as she had assumed? she thought angrily. And why should she care?

Carlotta rattled off a few sentences in rapid Spanish for Luke's ears only, though Robin didn't understand the language anyway. Luke evidently liked what she said, smiling into her dark eyes and kissing her on both cheeks before touching his mouth to hers. Robin turned away abruptly. He didn't have to be so blatant, so insensitive, as to flaunt his lover in front of her.

"Maybe we'll see each other again before you go back to England, Robin?" Carlotta said in that attractive voice of hers. "You must sample the ocean before you leave. It's still warm from summer. Maybe tomorrow morning, yes?"

"Maybe," Robin said, unable to say anything else. "It depends on Luke's plans. I'm only his secretary. . . ."

Carlotta's laugh was low and throaty and sexy.

"Of course, I was forgetting! Well, then, if you can't persuade Luke to let you have some time at the beach, I'll have to persuade him for you. It would be a shame if you didn't have time to enjoy this little bit of heaven!"

Luke laughed. "Get out of here, you little witch, and leave me to organise my own life! And for your information, Robin and I will be at the beach in the morning, okay?"

"Okay, darling." She ran her long, slender fingers around Luke's chin for a moment, blew Robin a kiss and was gone.

Robin felt furious at the implication that Carlotta could bend Luke to her will, while Robin, by her own admission, was merely his secretary. Why had she made herself sound so dull in front of the other girl, Robin thought in amazement? It wasn't like her at all, but then, ever since she had met Luke Burgess, she had been most unlike herself.

"Beautiful, isn't she?" Luke's voice broke into her thoughts. He was watching her, catlike.

"Yes, she is, if you like that type. Personally I find those dark Latin types rather too much."

My God, she was the catty one now, Robin thought, appalled. She realised Luke was laughing at her. At least he wasn't angry at her put-down of his girl friend. Her opinion probably wasn't important enough.

"Pity you didn't like her. She said some nice things about you."

"What things?" Robin asked suspiciously, remembering the stream of Spanish and Luke's pleased reaction. Surely that wasn't all on her account?

"She said what lovely golden hair you have—like sunlight, she called it. Those dark Latin types do get a bit poetic at times, don't they?"

"Did she really say that?" Robin stared at him, feeling ashamed of herself for the way she'd sneered at Carlotta.

Luke leaned forward and twisted a strand of her silky hair around his finger. "Would I lie to you? She was right, of course, but we dull Englishmen don't always manage to say the right words, do we?"

"You certainly don't." Robin pulled away from him. "Are you going to show me the island before we eat tonight? I don't want to come all this way and not see all of it. It's not very big, is it? I'd like a shower first."

"There's plenty of time. I'll leave you to it while I go and have a few words with Carlotta and check on the other villas. I'll be back for you in about half an hour, all right?"

"Lovely," she answered, and went quickly to her bedroom to sort out her clothes. If she was throwing him straight at Carlotta, it didn't matter. Nothing could have made Robin see more clearly that his life was different from hers. She didn't belong in it, except as far as business went. She made an impatient face at herself in the mirror and took her toilet things into the bathroom for a reviving shower.

Exactly half an hour later she was ready, wearing a cool green sun dress and carrying a light stole in case the evening got cooler later on. She heard Luke come into the villa while she was changing, and he, too, showered and changed in double-quick time. He looked virile and masculine in a black open-necked shirt and light-coloured slacks, a sweater tied casually round his neck. As they left the villa, the couple Robin had seen earlier were still engrossed in each other, lying languidly on an almost motionless sun-bed on the glassy blue water in the small curve of the bay.

"The honeymooners," Luke observed, following her glance. "Lost in a world of their own."

For some reason she wished he hadn't said that. Then she told herself not to be so silly and got in the car with him. It was incredible to think it was still only late afternoon, and there they were in Ibiza, following the same route back through Ibiza town and across to the other side of the island to take a look at the large resort of San Antonio with its hotel blocks and beautifully crystal-clear water lapping in the harbour.

"You'd see millions of tiny fish right up against the harbour wall if you got out and looked," Luke told her. "They're a tourist attraction in themselves. We'll get out if you like, but I thought we'd make this a whistle-stop tour around the coast, as I've booked us a meal on the other side."

"Oh, that's fine by me," Robin said. "I'm just loving it all, getting the flavour of it, if nothing else."

They drove up steeply winding cliff roads that took her breath away, into pine-scented hills and through farmland where the natives still looked as if they belonged to another era. They skirted magnificent coastal scenery with gigantic inaccessible cliffs and tiny villages with whitewashed houses and sparse brown fields that didn't look as if they supported any kind of commercial vegetation at all. There were so many changing faces of nature in such a small island.

Finally they stopped at a restaurant, seemingly perched on the cliff edge, overlooking the sea.

By then Robin had lost all sense of direction. She was still slightly disoriented from just being there, and when she said as much, Luke pointed out the curve of the coastline and told her the villas were around the next bend of the hills. They had done a full circle of the island in a couple of hours, and then Robin realised she was very hungry—more than ready to do justice to a marvellous seafood meal and the excellent local wine.

She relaxed at last. It was nearly impossible to do otherwise in that balmy atmosphere. It was dusk and the sky was beginning to be studded with myriad stars. A full yellow moon seemed to hang in midair, as if specially ordered to add to the enchantment of the island, and Robin caught her breath, ever sensitive to natural beauty.

For a second she remembered the honeymooners at the beach and felt a twist of envy at their completeness with one another. It seemed to cocoon them, even from where she watched them, high above in the villa. How wonderful to feel that close to someone. Her eyes were appreciating all she saw and slowly came round to Luke. As she focussed on his face her heart leapt at the look in his eyes. Unaware that he had been watching her, she surprised a look that for once was devoid of male aggression, a look that she couldn't readily define but that made her heart race and made her remember that she would keep her door locked that night. She was too vulnerable there, and he could be so charming when he set out to be . . . dangerously so.

After dinner they drove back to the villa, and Robin was pleasantly sleepy. The sound of the ocean far below the villa reminded her of home, and she thanked Luke sincerely for a lovely evening. She said good night and moved towards her room, but before she reached it he had barred her way, his arms imprisoning her, his face very close to hers. His intention was so plain that she gave a little gasp, suddenly wide awake.

"Luke, you promised," she said weakly.

He brushed that aside impatiently, and Robin felt as if her legs were turning to water. The wine they had had with dinner had been more potent than she had thought, and she had drunk rather a lot of it for Dutch courage. Now she knew it had been a mistake. Her mind was muddled, knowing that in spite of all the reasons why she would never submit to Luke, he was the most exciting man she had ever met.

And those reasons for not letting him make love to her were becoming decidedly hazy there in the warmth of his embrace, in that lovers' paradise.

"You weren't really going to bed without even one kiss, were you, Robin?" His voice was soft, huskily seductive, his mouth a whisper away from hers. She almost ached for him to take his one kiss and be done with it, but she knew it wouldn't end there. It wasn't going to end there. . . .

She heard herself give a melting sigh, and then she was winding her arms around him, feeling the taut strength in him as he held her tight. His mouth crushed hers, possessing hers, bruising its softness and forcing her willing lips apart as his tongue probed the inner warmth.

Her senses were aroused more fully than they had ever been before. There was no right or wrong, no loving or hating, only the glorious pleasure they were sharing. An explosion of emotion that was almost physical seemed to hold her in its grip, heightening every movement Luke made. She gloried in the feel of his mouth on hers, his arms holding her close, his fingers stroking her back as if he would know every inch of her spine, the long hard lines of his body wanting possession, totally demanding.

"I want you as I've never wanted any other woman, Robin," he said thickly against her mouth. "And you want me too. Tell me you want me. You'll stay here in my arms until you do."

"I want you, Luke," she said faintly. "And I want to stay in your arms."

He was confusing her with words. She wanted to stay there forever, held by him, wanted by him, and the needs he aroused in her were no less than his. He suddenly scooped her up in his arms as if she weighed nothing, strode across to her bedroom, carried her inside and kicked the door shut behind them both. He laid her down on the bed gently and stayed with her, the weight of him half covering her, as if these moments were too precious for him to leave her side even for a moment.

"Why have you been so stubborn all this time, my darling?" he whispered in her ear. "You must have known right from the beginning, as I did, that we were made for each other."

His fingers were unfastening the front buttons of her sun dress as he spoke, so subtly that she hardly knew it was happening until she felt the soft night air on her breasts and then Luke's caressing hands on them. Her breath caught in her throat at the intense pleasure the seductive little movements gave her, and then she felt the cool, damp touch of his tongue on her nipple, making her gasp out loud. He circled it gently, and hardly knowing that she did so, Robin moved her own hands inside the unbuttoned black shirt Luke wore; her fingers meshed into the dark body hair and caressed the flat male nipples. She heard him catch his breath at the action.

She neither knew nor cared how his shirt had

become undone. She was dizzy with the desire he aroused in her, needing him . . . wanting him. . . .

"Luke—"

"Don't talk, my darling. Don't spoil it with words. We don't need words, do we? Everything we need to say to one another is being said already, and your responses are all I ever hoped for. You're so beautiful, Robin, so very lovely."

Her sun dress was buttoned through to the hem, and when Luke unfastened the last of the buttons, there was only a wisp of bikini briefs separating his searching hands from the last warm secret core of her. His mouth trailed a loving course over her waist and abdomen, as if he would learn every bit of her body by heart. His hands caressed her hips, teasing and playing with the thin strips of material at the sides, driving her to an almost frenzied need. He kissed the gentle curve of her belly, his fingers tugging gently at the fabric. Her eyes closed. Lit by moonlight, her skin was golden, and she felt a rush of gladness that she looked beautiful for him. It was the first time she had ever felt that way, wanting to be perfect for a man. And the ultimate moment of giving and receiving love was so near—so spectacularly near. She could hear the raggedness of Luke's breathing and the thud of his heart, matching hers. She could feel his own arousal, and the culmination of desire was imminent.

Dimly, as if from another world, Robin heard the slam of a car door. Other people didn't exist. They didn't matter. All that mattered was that Luke was loving her, and she . . . she loved him so much. She knew it in one exquisite moment. She loved him, loved him . . . she would have told him so right then, but she realised that his attention had wandered, and the sound of footsteps crunching on the gravel outside was getting louder. It was impossible. Not now, not now!

Luke cursed furiously. Robin knew he hadn't locked the front door, and the light was still blazing in the lounge. Anyone might think they were still about. The next moment she heard Carlotta's lilting voice calling Luke's name and inviting them both to her villa for a nightcap.

"She won't leave now that she knows we're here," Luke muttered. "I'll try to get rid of her. Stay right there, darling. Don't move!"

He gave her a quick kiss and went swiftly out of the bedroom. Robin lay quite still, stunned for a moment. The cool night air that had felt so erotic moments ago now seemed to chill her as she heard the sound of voices from the lounge, Carlotta's husky and teasing, Luke's subdued. She couldn't hear the words they said, but the sound of their low laughter as they shared an intimate moment seared right through her.

Robin struggled to refasten her sun dress. She shook all over. Minutes earlier it had been with passion. Now it was with the appalling realisation that while she had so nearly confessed her love to Luke, love had never been one of the words he had used. He *wanted* her, lusted for her, but he didn't love her. She had been intoxicated with the wine and with Luke, but her mind was crystal clear now and was filled with deep, raw humiliation at the way he had nearly possessed her. He must have planned it all along, she raged inwardly. Playing on her love of the idyllic serenity of Cornwall, so akin to that corner of Ibiza. Playing on her emotions, her undeniable response to his masculine charisma.

Robin swung her feet out of bed and onto the soft carpeted floor. She was across the room in seconds, turning the key in the lock and leaning against the door, her soft lips trembling, tears shivering on her lashes. How close Luke had come to winning. Because that was all it was, of course: a seductive game in which he was determined to be the winner. Robin passed a shaking hand across her brow. It was damp with perspiration.

She jumped as she heard the front door close and the footsteps approach. Then the door handle turned, and her throat constricted as she imagined the incredulous look on Luke's face on the other side of the door. The egotism of the man was unbelievable! To send one girl away while he left another one waiting for him . . . or was Carlotta used to that kind of behaviour? Maybe she was the kind of girl who didn't mind if a man hopped from one bed to another, but Robin wasn't and never could be. Her hands clenched tightly at her sides as she heard Luke's voice.

"Open the door, darling."

"I wouldn't open it for you if you were the last man on earth," she heard herself scream as all the pent-up rage and hurt spilled over. "Don't you ever touch me again, do you hear? Get out of here and leave me alone!"

"Robin, for God's sake, open this door! I can't leave you like this." He sounded angry then, as if the two of them had never been almost as close as two people could possibly be.

"Well, you'd better, because I don't want to see you again tonight," she shouted back. "Can't you understand? I hate you. I want to be left alone!"

For a minute she wondered if he'd push the door in. He was strong enough and capable enough, and Robin felt a flicker of fear. The next second she heard his voice, cold as ice.

"Then that's exactly what you'll be. I shan't disturb you again."

She heard the slam of the front door as he left the villa, and she didn't need to be a genius to guess where he'd gone for consolation. She stood numbly for a few minutes more, then undressed quickly and slid beneath the thin bedcover. Let him go to Carlotta —what did she care! But when the numbness wore off and the hurt became a physical reality, Robin knew she did care, very deeply.

In the quiet of the night she imagined she could hear the soft, throaty sounds of laughter drifting back on the still air from Carlotta's villa. She imagined her and Luke together. She thought of the honeymoon couple, oblivious to all else but each other on that romantic night, and of the other occupants of the villas, happy in their own private worlds. Suddenly Robin felt more alone than she had ever done in her life. The grief she had felt over Elaine Fowler's death was quite different from this. To discover the truth about herself now—that what she felt for Luke was love, deeply passionate, once-and-forever love—and then to have it thrown back in her face, was too much for her to take.

She buried her face beneath the bedcovers and wept. It didn't matter one iota that Luke had gone to someone else or that he might have had a legion of women before her. Painfully, Robin was learning that love took no account of the mismatching of personalities, and no matter how much she wanted the hate to remain uppermost in her mind, the fact remained that she loved him. And until he truly loved her, which was as likely as hell freezing, her own love was destined to remain sterile and unfulfilled.

Somehow, exhausted, Robin finally slept. She didn't hear Luke come back to the villa. She didn't even know if he came back at all. Pale and heavy-eyed next morning, she showered quickly, not certain what she should do next. Still in her robe as she came out of the bathroom, she encountered Luke's hard, unsmiling gaze. Her heart jolted. He wore black swimming trunks and nothing else, and her face flamed at the sight of the hair-roughened chest in which she had raked her fingers the night before. Last night seemed a hundred light-years ago. . . .

"There's toast and coffee in the kitchen if you want it," he said in a clipped voice. "I suggest we spend a couple of hours on the beach, since it's a shame to waste this sun. Carlotta will meet us there and has invited us to lunch at her villa. We'll fly straight back to England afterwards."

It was easy to see that his male ego was badly bruised after her rejection of him the previous night. But what had he expected? What woman wouldn't have reacted the way she had? Robin thought wildly. She tried not to look at the lean, hard, tanned body and remember the way it had felt against hers. She looked somewhere over the top of his head, her chin tilted defiantly, but in reality she was still very close to tears.

"That sounds fine by me," she said. Then she hesitated. This, after all, was her love. A little rush of emotion made her blurt out more than she intended. "Luke, about last night—"

"The less said about last night the better," he said, cutting her short. "It's over and forgotten. Let's concentrate on today, shall we?"

That said it all. He'd had one of his rare failures with her, and he wasn't a man to brood on it. There were always others. There was Carlotta. Later, when the three of them were stretched out on the golden sand, Robin realised how cruel Luke could be. It was her choice to reject him, and in all honesty he'd had every reason to expect her submission, so she could hardly blame him for making her feel that she was the third corner of a triangle.

Carlotta's voluptuous figure, bronzed to perfection with assistance of the suntan lotion she asked Luke to rub into her skin while she purred with pleasure, was causing Robin acute embarrassment as well as sheer agony. He was doing this on purpose, she thought heatedly, he was paying her back, yet he was doing nothing immoral or outrageous. It was Robin's own extrasensitive perceptions that caused her the most pain. Even when he offered to rub the lotion into Robin's skin, too, she refused coldly, saying she would manage herself, for how could she bear the seductive caress of his palms on her flesh and not remember?

Somehow she got through the morning and the cold-meat-and-salad lunch at Carlotta's villa. Somehow she behaved as pleasantly as she could, considering that her heart was breaking into little pieces every time she saw the warm glances that passed between the other two. Yesterday she might have sneered as she saw Luke operate . . . but that was yesterday, before she had admitted to herself that she loved him.

Chapter Ten

It was a relief to be on the plane, flying back to England, and even more of a relief when Luke dropped Robin off at her flat. They had spent a mostly silent and uneasy afternoon together, and once alone, Robin wilted, feeling just like a rubber band that had lost all its elasticity. The following day she would be back in the office, and Luke would be going up north to look at another prospective site. Would there be some other client with a pretty daughter to tempt him? she thought bitterly.

But the bitterness was only temporary, because the pain of her situation was still too searingly new to be thought about lightly. She was no coquette, content to flit about from one man to the next, but a warm, passionate woman, capable of giving to one man all her most tender and ardent loving. And the one man she wanted in all the world was as careless with his affections as if he were merely tossing away a candy wrapper. For Robin it wasn't enough. In a moment of bittersweet regret, she dearly wished that it was. To take what Luke offered—the pleasures of the flesh, as heady as wine, but without that essential ingredient of mutual love—would be meaningless. Such a relationship would end only in heartbreak for Robin, triumph for Luke. Better to have nothing, nothing at all.

They were noble thoughts, but in the soft, cold darkness of an English night, they didn't warm her as Luke's arms had warmed her. Many sleepless, troubled hours passed before Robin told herself not to be such a fool. If Luke saw how affected she was by all that had happened, he'd still have won. He'd see that she was a vulnerable woman, as susceptible as any of them to his charms, whether she gave in to them or not. And she was too spirited to let that happen, too much a survivor to let him think he had that much power over her. Gradually her determination not to let him see how deeply hurt she had been by his attentions to Carlotta after her own near-seduction overcame Robin's distress. At last she fell into an exhausted sleep.

The next day at the office, Robin was disgusted to find that Maureen and Sonia had put quite a different interpretation on her trip with Luke.

"Where did he take you, Robin?" Maureen said at once. "Somewhere exotic, I bet. The Algarve in Portugal or the complex in Capri? And was it fabulous, you lucky thing? What I'd give if Luke Burgess would take me off for a romantic couple of days, but I don't think I'm his type."

She sighed with mock envy, patting her ample curves. Robin put her right at once, her green eyes flashing out warnings that the other two had better believe her.

"It wasn't a romantic trip, I assure you! It was business."

Sonia hooted disbelievingly.

"Tell that to the Marines, Robin. With your looks and style, our Luke would have had only one thing in mind!"

Robin gave her a freezing look that would have silenced anybody else but the thick-skinned Sonia.

"Well, you can just forget it, all right? Nothing happened—not the way you mean, anyway. We went to Ibiza, and it was very nice, and I went to see the complex, that's all. I don't want to hear another word about it."

She marched into her office and began riffling papers about angrily. She was more upset than she let on, because what they surmised had not only nearly happened, she had *wanted* it to happen, very much, before Carlotta's untimely arrival, saving her from a fate worse than death, she thought cynically. She knew that if she relaxed her guard for a second, her wayward dreaming could take her right back to that moonlit room where Luke's powerful body had sought to possess hers, and she had wanted to give it to him with no thought to tomorrow.

And now it was tomorrow, and the warmth of Ibiza was only a memory in the cold English drizzle of a late October day. There was work to be done, and Robin plunged herself into it gladly. It was preferable to thinking and dreaming. She was so thankful that Luke was away for a few days, but she needn't have worried, because when he did return to Bristol he hardly came near the office, phoning in any messages. When he finally appeared his face was cold and remote.

There was an obstacle in his way on the northern deal, and Luke Burgess was a man who was determined to overcome all obstacles. As his secretary, of course, Robin was kept aware of what was happening. As the woman who loved him, she ached to take the strain out of his face when the deal threatened to fall through. But that was something she wouldn't dare to do at the present time.

Besides, she had her own worries. She felt increasingly unwell all that week, refusing to give in to the feeling, although Maureen told her how peaky she looked, Robin could have told her that her heavy-eyed look had less to do with the aching limbs and streaming cold that came on strong by the end of the week than a more basic anguish. But finally she gave in and went back to the flat at lunchtime on Friday. It wasn't fair to the others to remain in the office. Luke was still battling with his northern client, and Robin intended to hibernate in her flat for the weekend, dosing herself up with aspirins and hot lemonade and coddling herself with hot-water bottles and a cocoon of blankets.

She was miserable, aching in every part of her, staggering out of bed now and then to make a hot drink or a bowl of soup or a sandwich. She didn't feel like eating anything, and only did so out of habit and to keep up what little strength she still had. She didn't want somebody coming in there and finding a wasted corpse in the bed, she thought weakly. And she had to be well by Monday. She had every intention of going into the office. She'd agreed to work for Luke until the Cornish complex was finished, and she wouldn't go back on her word, no matter what it cost her to continue seeing him.

She drifted in and out of sleep the entire weekend, sometimes waking up in a drenched tangle of bedclothes from a nightmare, other times floating sweetly into Luke's arms, dreaming that he loved her, that all the bitterness between them was over and only a golden future was before them. Sometimes the dreams were shamefully erotic, and always it was Luke's hands that held and caressed her, Luke's mouth that kissed her and roused her to heights of ecstacy, Luke who whispered against her mouth the words of love she had never heard from him.

Always, when she awoke after such a dream, tears would be filling her eyes. Maybe she would drown in her own tears, she thought vaguely. Maybe she was going crazy. There were other voices in her head now, low and deep, unrecognisable, except one of them.

"She's waking up now," Luke said, his voice tight with anxiety. Robin turned her head a fraction of an inch as the swirling mists cleared a little. Luke was kneeling by the bed, and a strange man was holding her wrist.

"How long has she been like this?" the stranger said.

"I found her only this morning when I came to take her to the office. I phoned to tell my receptionist I wouldn't be in and was told that Robin had gone home sick on Friday. I assume she's been here all weekend."

It was like watching a play: No one was asking her, even though she was the principal character. Her throat felt so swollen that she doubted if she could have answered them anyway, but she managed to nod at Luke's words. She felt the sting of a needle in her arm as the doctor gave her an injection. She felt as useless as a rag doll.

"Influenza with a touch of pneumonia," she heard the doctor say. "I should have been sent for sooner. She shouldn't be here by herself."

"My house is across the green," Luke said at once. "If she's well wrapped, can I drive her there? My housekeeper and I will look after her."

The doctor nodded. "Good. She'll need watching for at least two weeks. She's got no resistance, from the look of her. I'll give you a prescription and I'll look in on her tonight at your house, Mr. Burgess. I'll see her into your car before I go."

She had no say in it. She wanted to protest, to argue, to say she couldn't possibly stay at Luke's house, giving him and Mrs. Somerton so much trouble, but the words wouldn't come. After the doctor's injection she was starting to float again, retreating into that other world that usually ended in black oblivion. The last thing she remembered was being wrapped in blankets and being held close to Luke's chest. His arms were strong, and hers were so weak, so weak. . . .

The days passed in a haze. Robin knew she was in an unfamiliar bed in unfamiliar surroundings. Faces came and went, vaguely registered in her mind: the doctor, Mrs. Somerton and Luke. So many times when she threshed about in her fever there were strong hands to hold her, hands that gave her strength, that smoothed the tangled hair from her hot forehead, that cooled her cheeks with cologne-scented cloths and the occasional kiss. Luke . . . Luke . . . always there.

On her first really lucid day she awoke alone, trying to piece together the fragments of disjointed sentences—trying to decide whether she had really heard him talk her through her fever, badgering her to get well—not in any antagonistic way, but anxiously, calling her his darling, his love.

Her bedroom door opened and he came in, dressed for the office. Robin's cheeks flushed, knowing she had been on the brink of fantasising once more, and this Luke was the same as ever, the slightly mocking look in his eyes tempered by relief.

"Well, it looks as if you've finally come back to us, Robin," he said easily, with no hint of emotion, no inflexion in his voice that indicated she was special to him. Nothing. She swallowed thickly.

"How long have I been here?" she asked, her voice still husky with sleep. There was a gnawing emptiness in her stomach, and she had no idea whether she had eaten in hours or days. It felt like an eternity.

"A week," Luke said abruptly. "And you'll stay here another week on doctor's orders."

"I—I can't." She struggled to sit up, feeling the room swim, and sinking back on the pillows. "I'm being too much trouble, Luke."

"Don't be ridiculous. Do you think I'd let you go back to your own flat in that weakened state? I owe it to your father to look after you, since it was my idea to bring you here. I feel responsible for you."

And that was all! The sharp way he spoke made Robin bite her trembling lips. She was nothing to him, other than the daughter of his business partner. All that sweet seduction in the villa in Ibiza had been no more than his natural reaction to being alone with an attractive woman. He'd made no secret of his desire, but there was nothing more. The pain of it was searing.

"Does my father know I've been ill?" She had to think of other things before she fell apart in front of him. She didn't know this tall, dark stranger who looked down at her so remotely. Had she imagined all the tenderness the week before? Had it all been a hallucination after all? Robin could have wept at the thought.

"I phoned James as soon as I'd brought you here," he told her, still brusque. "He would have come to see you, but we had the doctor's assurance that the worst was probably over, so I've been giving James nightly bulletins on your condition. There's a phone by your bed. Please use it to call him as soon as you feel able."

The rough consideration made her swallow tightly again.

"Luke, I want to thank you—"

"Then do it by getting well and doing as you're told.

Mrs. Somerton will be glad to see that your eyes are clear at last and back to their usual ferocity." This time his face relaxed into a brief smile. "All those invalid foods she's been concocting to tempt you have been wasted!"

"I don't remember any of them," Robin confessed, and then she made a face. "Anyway, they won't be wasted today, but invalid foods sound ghastly. I feel as if I could eat a horse, I'm so ravenous!"

He leaned forward and kissed her lightly on the cheek, his voice filled with laughter.

"That's my girl! Though I'm sure Mrs. Somerton will dream up something more palatable than that. I have to go now, but I'll see you tonight. If you think you can stop being so lazy, maybe you can come downstairs to dinner. I've got quite tired of carrying you about."

He breezed out of the room, and Robin felt her cheeks flame. Just how much of a liability had she been in the past week? She didn't want to dwell on it, and minutes later Mrs. Somerton came into the room with a loaded breakfast tray, smiling with relief to see her charge looking more like her old self.

They were so kind, both of them, Robin thought, with a rush of gratitude. The motives didn't matter; the concern was there. This was confirmed an hour later when she dialled her home number and heard her father's well-loved voice at the other end. Once the preliminaries were over and he was assured that she was recovering, his words were more revealing than Luke's.

"I've never heard anyone so worried, darling," James said. "He covered it well for my benefit, of course, and although I thought I should be there, he insisted there was no danger and only loving care was needed, and you were getting the best of that."

"Mrs. Somerton has been wonderful," Robin said.

"I'm not talking about Mrs. Somerton. Don't underestimate Luke's part in all this, Robin. He blames himself for some reason, though the doctor says it was a combination of many things that caused the complications. Luke told him something about you, and the diagnosis was that you were in a weakened nervous state after Mrs. Fowler's death and hadn't fully got over that before you were plunged into the new crisis down here. I hadn't realised just how deeply you resented it all, darling, until Luke explained it."

"Don't go blaming yourself, Dad. And I've never thought of myself as a weak, nervous person. For heaven's sake! It was more likely to be coming back to rainy old England after those two lovely days on Ibiza that did it. It was only flu."

James laughed. "It wasn't only flu, and you know it by now. But I can hear that you're back in form, so I'll stop worrying about you. Why don't you come down here to convalesce?"

"I don't think so, Dad. I'd rather get back to work as soon as I can. I shall really feel like an invalid if I need to convalesce."

"Then promise me you'll have at least a week down here at Christmas, Robin. Luke can spare you for that time, and it wouldn't be Christmas if we weren't together."

"All right, Dad," she said softly before she hung up.

Later that day she sat up in a chair while Mrs. Somerton changed her sheets. She was told that on the other times this had happened, Luke had carried her to the chair and held her there until her bed was ready again.

"You've both been so kind," she said, her breath catching a little. "I'd never have expected Luke to be so patient with illness."

"He had a lot of practise when his mother was ill, dear," Mrs. Somerton told her. "She was a lovely person, and Luke was devoted to her. He spent many hours reading to her in her last weeks. He has far more patience than people give him credit for. It stands him in good stead in his business dealings too. He'll chip away at something he wants until he gets it."

For the first time in days Robin felt a renewed suspicion of Luke. Guiltily so, because he had been more than generous in looking after her and putting his house at her disposal, but all the same she decided there was no way she would be carried down to dinner that evening. She would be dressed and downstairs long before he was due home. The instinct for self-preservation was already back, and Robin knew she was on the mend.

She stayed at Luke's house another week, but it was a relief to go back to her own place. Often, Luke had to go out after dinner, and on two nights he hadn't come home for dinner at all, saying he had business to attend to. Robin had too much pride to ask what that business was. Why should he want to spend any more of his time with his secretary, anyway, when he probably had far more agreeable companions with whom to spend his time? She tormented herself by imagining it, but she forced herself to face reality. It was futile to pine over what might have been.

Naturally he looked in to see her in her own flat quite often before she was declared fit enough to return to the office, nearly three weeks later. During that time, Mrs. Somerton had popped in to do the cleaning and some of the cooking, until Robin felt she had been pampered long enough.

"It's got to stop, Luke," she protested when he came to the flat one night with an armful of flowers exquisitely wrapped in florist's paper. "They're beautiful, but I don't deserve this treatment!"

"That's a matter of opinion," he said dryly. "Anyway, these aren't from me. They're from the staff. Take a look at the card if you don't believe me."

Robin flushed with pleasure as she saw that it was true, though she suspected that Luke had put a substantial amount to the collection himself to account for the lovely arrangement.

"It's wonderful of them, and I'm touched that they care about me enough to bother. *Everyone* has been wonderful, and if you don't get out of here, I'm going to get all emotional again and I absolutely refuse to cry one more tear!" She gave a forced laugh, and Luke saw the determined little tilt to her chin. She saw the familiar male arrogance come into his blue eyes. She had forgotten just how blue they were. They reminded her of the sea beneath the villa in Ibiza, and were ridiculously beautiful for a man, the lashes fringing them long and straight, but in no way effeminate. That was one word that could never be applied to Luke Burgess. Robin tore her gaze away from him.

"You get more like your old self every day, darling," he taunted lightly. "The spikes are already appearing."

"You'll know you'd better keep your distance then, won't you?" Robin retorted, glad to be sparring with him again, because it was easier on her nerves that way. As if to prove to her that he could still dominate her, he was suddenly at her side and pulling her into his arms.

She was more slender now after her illness, fitting snugly into his embrace. She had no time to protest before his mouth sought the sweetness of hers in a kiss that was tender and lingering. It took her so much by surprise after Luke's more passionate assaults on her senses that for endless moments she could only register the warm, pleasurable sensations the contact gave her, all resistance gone.

Then he removed his mouth from hers, still keeping her in the circle of his arms. Robin's eyes slowly opened, and the eyes looking into hers were amused.

"Don't tempt me, Robin," he said softly. "Maybe you don't remember how many times you clung to me when you were ill, or how often it was only my voice that seemed to calm you or my touch you needed. You're not always so averse to my presence."

She thrust herself away from him, her eyes blazing with fury. He was beneath contempt to throw that up at her now, and the knowledge that it hadn't all been a dream, that he had been there whenever she needed him, filled her with nothing but humiliation at that moment.

"You're absolutely loathsome, Luke." She spat out the words, her voice low and controlled. "To take advantage of me when I was half delirious is just about the most despicable thing I can imagine."

"I didn't *take advantage* of you, as you so quaintly put it, you little idiot," Luke said angrily, all softness gone. His arms dropped from around her and she stepped back, as if she couldn't be far enough from him. "What do you think would have happened to you if I hadn't come and found you that morning?"

"I don't know, and right now I don't care! I've told you I'm grateful to you and Mrs. Somerton, but that's got nothing to do with here and now, has it? I may have been weak in body, but I'm not weak in the head, and if you think you're going to use some kind of blackmail over me to seduce me—"

"My God, do you think I have to resort to blackmail to make love to a woman?"

"You don't know the meaning of the word *love,*" Robin raged at him.

She saw him go rigid, and for a moment she thought

she had gone too far. Luke looked ready to strike her, the muscles tight in his face, his whole attitude one of lean, hard aggression, his mouth a compressed line of anger.

"And neither do you," he flung at her before he stomped out.

Chapter Eleven

Once back at work, Robin realised that Luke had taken to heart her request for him to keep his distance: not physically, because there were many times when they were together, including his driving her to and from the office when he wasn't out of town; but mentally they were poles apart now, and to Robin it was almost unbelievable that they had ever been close.

Almost. But in the silence of the night, when she was unable to keep up the brittle facade, her control slipped a little. Her subconscious refused to let her forget the time she had spent in Luke's arms at the villa, how beautiful it had been, how right and natural. Then he had been, and still was, all she had ever wanted in a man, all she had ever dreamed of. But he didn't love her, and her own pride wouldn't let her accept anything less.

She wished she could be less rigid in her thinking, able to accept an affair for what it was, an enjoyable interlude with no harm done on either side. But she wasn't made that way, and her feelings ran far too deep. She could only be thankful she had come to her senses in time at the villa, for by now she would have been even more unhappy, having once known the ultimate pleasure of Luke's love.

Her mouth twisted in the darkness every time that word came to her mind. It wasn't love. And his final taunt at her flat that she didn't know the meaning of it, either, was the bitterest irony of all.

He had agreed to her taking a week off for Christmas, and as the time grew near, Robin eagerly looked forward to it. Relaxing at Pollard Manor with her father was just the therapy she needed. She thought of her love for Luke more as a sickness requiring therapy than the physical illness from which she had recovered. With James and familiar surroundings, and all that home meant, she hoped to put everything in perspective and leave all this madness behind her. Nothing was impossible.

Before she left, insisting on taking the train, even though Luke offered to drive her, he gave her a small package wrapped in shiny silver paper, telling her not to open it until Christmas Day. Robin felt acutely embarrassed at the gift. Although she and the girls in the office had exchanged presents, she had merely arranged for a huge floral basket to be delivered to Luke's house for him and Mrs. Somerton. It wouldn't be there until Christmas Eve.

Seeing her flushed face, Luke spoke gruffly. "Don't worry. I always give my secretaries a present at Christmas."

"Then, thank you, Luke," she said sincerely. "And thanks for bringing me to the station."

He'd got her there just in time, leaving no time for prolonged good-byes, to Robin's relief. He'd handed her the package at the station. She hoped desperately he wouldn't kiss her. All around them, couples seemed to be embracing as the train doors were shutting, and she got inside quickly, putting the door between them. He caught her hand, squeezing it for a moment.

"I think I'd better go, Robin. I'm due on site in half an hour. Have a good Christmas, and give my regards to James. I'll phone you sometime."

Suddenly he was gone, swallowed up in the crowds, as if business were more urgent than standing there on a cold and windy station platform. Robin turned away, her heart thudding painfully, wishing things could have been different between them, her eyes misting as she found her seat in the train and buried her head in a paperback novel to avoid making conversation with other passengers.

She felt ridiculously as if she were leaving her heart behind, leaving all that she loved in that dark retreating figure who didn't care the way she cared. Then she remembered her father and knew fervently that there was one person who truly loved her and had never let her down. For the moment she completely forgot that it had been James's business deal with Luke that had triggered off her meeting with him. James was the haven to which she was returning with a heavy heart.

He met her at the station after the long journey west, and Robin was instantly comforted by the familiar warmth of his embrace. The few unavoidable tears were explained away by the aftereffects of her illness, though she assured him she was fine now.

"You're thinner," James observed when they were back at the manor and drinking a welcome cup of tea and sampling some of Mrs. Drew's homemade fruitcake. "It doesn't suit you, Robin. Mrs. Drew will soon fatten you up with her Christmas delicacies!"

"You make me sound more like the Christmas turkey." She laughed, her eyes suspiciously bright at the anxiety she still saw in him. "I don't want fattening up, Dad. I like being thinner! Some women pay good money at a health farm to achieve what I did in a couple of weeks."

But she knew that she wasn't fooling him one bit; he knew her too well. When he ruffled her gleaming hair as he used to do when she was a child, she knew just how near to the surface her emotions were as she forced down the lump in her throat. She was as vulnerable as the child she had once been.

"Well, whatever you say, darling, you'll be taken good care of now—though I think Luke and his housekeeper did a marvellous job, didn't they? He phoned me twice a day, you know, morning and evening."

"Did he?" Robin hadn't known that. "That must have alarmed you even more."

"Not at all. I was exceedingly grateful to him. He thinks a great deal of you, Robin. I half hoped that you and he—"

"You can forget any matchmaking ideas, Dad. He's a good and generous boss, and I admit that I was wrong about the complex spoiling the environment if it's to be anything like the one we went to in Ibiza—"

"How was that?" James changed the conversation quickly, as her voice had become heated. If he thought she rose to the bait unnecessarily, he had his own ideas as to the reasons. "You didn't say much about it when you phoned to tell me you were back, and then you were ill. Was it as tasteful as Luke has always insisted, blending in with the natural scenery?"

"Oh, yes. I couldn't fault him on that." Her voice became toneless. She didn't trust herself, not wanting to think about Ibiza too deeply. Instead she spoke of the development from a purely professional viewpoint. "Luke was quite right when he said he wouldn't ravage the landscape. The villas look as if they'd sprung up out of the hillside perfectly naturally, and the screen of trees is as effective as he said. He has an eye for it, I'll agree to that."

She wouldn't be drawn any further, except on superficial comments about the complex. Her attitude troubled James very much, but he knew Robin to be as stubborn as a mule when she wanted to be. And if she and Luke were having some kind of problems, it wasn't for him to interfere. It wouldn't hurt to give nature a helping hand, though, he decided thoughtfully.

During the few days leading up to Christmas, Robin drove into Helston to buy last-minute items for the tree and in general to get herself into the Christmas mood, difficult though it seemed. There was a block of ice around her heart, and she missed Luke more than she would have thought possible. Even the wrangling between them had been stimulating in its way. Now, there was nothing but blankness.

He had phoned her once, but the conversation had been stilted. She couldn't converse naturally with him, and she had been his secretary for too short a time for them to have any long-standing business topics to discuss. She was almost glad when he hung up, and then immediately longed for the sound of his voice once more.

She had held back the tears as they finished speaking and told her father abruptly that she was going out for a while. It was early evening, the day before Christmas Eve, and Robin got in her car and drove aimlessly along the coast with its grey, gaunt cliffs and foaming sea, through little towns and villages where Christmas-tree lights shone out from cottage windows. Occasionally she saw groups of carol singers, their messages of love and goodwill seeming a mockery of her. Never had she felt so dispirited.

When she got back to the manor, James poured out two glasses of sherry and handed one to her as she rubbed her cold hands together. Her face was pinched, the skin drawn tightly over her bones. She was as lovely as ever, but with an ethereal look about her that alarmed James more than he let her know.

"What's this for?" she asked him. "Are we celebrating Christmas two days early? You don't usually indulge until just before dinner."

"We're celebrating the fact that we're having a guest for Christmas to cheer up our lonely twosome," James said.

"A guest?" Robin wasn't too sure about that. She wasn't in the mood for making polite small talk. She'd thought her father appreciated that. "Who is it? Anyone I know?"

The minute she asked the question, she knew. James's voice had been just too casual, and she put down her glass, slopping some of the golden liquid.

"Now, before you go off half cocked, this is my house and I'll invite who I like to stay in it." James spoke fast, seeing the outrage in her eyes. "It's time you and Luke got this damn nonsense sorted out between you, whatever it is, and I don't need a crystal ball to tell me something's wrong! I phoned him back when you'd gone out and asked him down here. He'll be arriving tomorrow afternoon, and then the two of you can travel back together in his car the day after Boxing Day. And *don't argue,* Robin!"

He used the same tone he had used when she was a child, and suddenly all the anger was crumbling away and she was in his arms, being comforted by his soothing voice, her entire frame shaking as she sobbed against his chest.

"Why don't you tell me what's wrong, Robin?" James said gently. "You always came to me with your secrets, didn't you? Remember?"

"Grown-up secrets are different," she mumbled. "This is something I have to work out for myself, Dad. Just be around if I need you, that's all I ask."

"I always have been, haven't I?" He kissed her hot cheek, smoothing back her hair, reminding her of how Luke had done the same thing when she had been ill.

"What time did Luke say he'd be here?" she asked huskily.

"Oh, mid-afternoon sometime. You won't run out on us, will you, darling? It's useless to try and run away from problems. All you do is delay the moment when you have to face up to them, and it *is* Christmas. Goodwill to all men and all that!"

He tried to cheer her up, and Robin gave a watery smile.

"Don't worry, I won't upset everybody. I'm just surprised Luke's coming down here. I'd have thought he had plenty of places in which to spend Christmas. I know his housekeeper's going to stay with some relatives for a couple of days, but Luke's not a man to go short of invitations."

"He obviously preferred our company," James replied.

There were times when he'd have loved to knock their two heads together if they couldn't see what was so obvious to him. He'd seen it when they came down to look over the site. The old cliché that love was blind was never truer than when applied to Robin and Luke, and if James could help things along a little, he'd go all out to do so.

Robin spent a restless night. Christmas was a family time and sometimes an emotional time. She could have done without Luke's company right then. She was still trying to sort herself out, and his presence wasn't going to help one bit. But James thought he was doing the right thing, and for her father's sake she would try to make the holiday an untraumatic one. By the time Luke's car arrived the next afternoon, she was sufficiently calm to go out and meet him, despite the fact that her heart was thumping.

He looked at her warily, not knowing how she ached with love for him, as if he expected a mini-explosion as soon as she got near him. Some reputation she had, Robin thought wryly. Instead she forced a smile and held out her hand.

"Thank you for coming. It means a lot to Dad, Luke. And it would mean a lot to me if we could call a truce."

"Another one?" But he was smiling, too, and his fingers curled around hers in unspoken agreement. Then he hauled his suitcase out of the car, the same one he'd taken to Ibiza. And there was also a flight bag, in which were some bottles of whisky and other spirits for James as a thank you for the invitation.

"I thought you'd be otherwise occupied," Robin said, trying not to make it sound too sneering, in view of her suggestion of a truce.

Luke answered lightly, "I decided that since it was impossible to choose between all the women fighting over me, I'd settle for you, darling. I know where I am with you, don't I?"

She glared at him for a minute, and then saw that he was teasing her.

"I suppose I deserved that," she admitted.

Luke laughed. "You did. Come on, let's get inside. It's chilly out here, and I must say, this feels almost like coming home. Christmas can be a lonely business."

That was something she'd never expected to hear Luke say, but Robin suddenly remembered the way

Mrs. Somerton had spoken of his deep affection for his mother. Robin didn't know how long ago she had died, but there was something about the note of sadness in Luke's voice just then that told her unerringly that he was thinking about her.

It subdued her tension a little, and with her father's determination to make this a real old-fashioned Christmas, the time passed more pleasurably than Robin had ever dreamed it would. Mrs. Drew had been with the family a long time and joined them for Christmas dinner as always, leaving them to the traditional present-opening around the tree after they had watched the Queen's TV transmission.

Robin had hastily bought Luke a present upon learning that he was coming to Cornwall. Hardly knowing what to buy for the man who had everything, she'd had sudden inspiration in a small bookshop and bought him a leather-bound edition on architecture through the ages, in which he was passionately interested.

She hadn't been tempted to open the small package he had given her at the railway station, pushing it to the bottom of her suitcase. But now he waited for her to open it with the rest of her gifts beneath the Christmas tree. Her hands shook a little as she took out the small jeweller's box, and then she gasped as she saw the exquisite little emerald earrings inside.

"I thought they'd be a good match for your mother's necklace," Luke said evenly.

She was startled that he had remembered it and was touched by the thought—and a bit perturbed, too, that the earrings must have cost far more than the kind of present a man usually gave to office staff. But that wasn't the moment to say so. She thanked him, her eyes glowing like the emeralds, leaving him in no doubt about her pleasure.

"Is that all the thanks I'm getting?" he asked, "when you're sitting right beneath a bunch of mistletoe?"

Before she could resist, he had moved towards her and pulled her to her feet and into his arms. Her own went around him automatically, and his mouth was warm on hers, and she felt all the tingling little shafts of pleasure his kiss always gave her. She couldn't push him away without appearing priggish, and this was only a kiss under the mistletoe. Nobody took them seriously!

Luke opened his present and was obviously delighted with it, insisting on another kiss. If that went on much longer, her nerves would be ragged, Robin thought weakly.

"I think it's time I made a discreet withdrawal," she heard James say, his voice seeming to come from a long distance. "Mrs. Drew is ready to go home to her family for the afternoon, so I'll take her now. I'll be back in an hour. I'm sure you two have plenty to say to each other without me around."

Robin looked up in alarm, but what James suggested was a long-standing arrangement and nothing unusual. And if she began arguing, it would look as if she were afraid to be alone with Luke. The implications of the thought were disturbing, but there was nothing she could do to keep her father from leaving with Mrs. Drew. When they arrived at the housekeeper's daughter's home, Robin knew he would be made welcome with a Christmas drink and would be expected to stay a short while. She ran her tongue around her dry lips as the sound of James's car faded in the distance.

She hardly dared look at Luke. It all seemed such a setup, and it was one she hadn't wanted. Maybe he thought she did. She spoke jerkily.

"Do you feel like a walk? It's such a lovely afternoon. The coast path might be a bit bracing, but I feel the need to walk off that huge meal, don't you?"

Please don't twist my words and say you have other needs that are more urgent, Robin pleaded inside her head. She just couldn't cope with it. Luke rose at once, holding out his hand to pull her to her feet. She held herself tense, wanting and yet resisting the certainty that he was going to pull her into his arms. When he didn't, she felt the sting of disappointment. Had she become so mixed up about the man that she even welcomed the battles rather than the platonic relationship she had demanded? Her thoughts were as capricious as the wind.

"It's a very good idea," Luke said briskly. "We can take a look at how the site is coming along too. They'll have made good progress with the reasonable weather lately."

It was just as if he had never stunned her senses with his seductive lovemaking at the villa, as if he was determined to keep strictly to their boss/secretary roles, since she had insisted on it. It was easier on her before she fell in love with him. She still wasn't sure why he was even here! Surely he could have spent Christmas with one of his women friends. She was convinced he had plenty, and Carlotta's hot, smouldering looks on the little beach on that last morning in Ibiza had left Robin no doubt that there was a very close relationship between them. If Carlotta didn't even care when Luke brought another woman to the island, it made Robin question very much just what that relationship was. It hinted at something very bohemian, and the kind of situation Robin simply couldn't take.

They wrapped up warmly and set out for the afternoon walk. The air was crisp and cold, and

Cornwall was in one of its most dramatic moods, windswept and gloriously wild, and Robin loved it. The wind tore at their hair and cut through their voices, but there was a primitive freedom about the elements that invigorated her. For a while all personal problems were reduced to insignificance, submerged in the glories of nature.

Luke held her hand, but it was companionship and not passion that tightened his grip, the need of one human being for another in appreciating the majestic forces at work there: crashing seas foaming against gaunt black cliffs; tall grasses and bracken yielding to the wind; the scent of the ocean as it rushed into sandy coves and inlets. Cornwall, land of legends, home. . . .

Robin felt an odd pricking in her eyes. She might have voiced her thoughts to Luke then, tremulously and revealingly, had the wind not carried the words away. And besides, by then they had neared the building site, and his thoughts were elsewhere, on practical, material things now, and the moment was gone.

"Quite a difference since you saw it last, isn't there?" Luke yelled in her ear. "It's starting to make sense now, and you can see the similarity to the complex in Ibiza."

Robin nodded. Her throat constricted a little. Clearly, Ibiza hadn't meant the same to him as it had to her, except that for a while he had been furious at the insult to his ego when she had locked him out of her bedroom. It proved her point, she told herself tightly.

"You see the stepped shape where the villas will be built?" Luke still had to shout right in her ear to make himself heard above the roar of the wind. "And the ample spaces for the trees for the necessary seclusion?

The only concession we shall have to make is a proper concrete flight of steps leading to the beach, so that our guests won't break their legs getting down there, but all that will be adequately screened too. But I don't need to explain all this, do I? You've seen the plans, and now that you've seen the other complex, you must agree that your first objections were unjustified."

His voice was confident, powerful. He had known all along that he could override any objections. Hers were of little importance anyway, since Luke was her father's business partner in this project. Robin's wishes had never entered into it. She felt oddly deflated, seeing Luke at that moment as implacable as the gaunt black cliffs that bent the ocean with their fortresslike solidity. As Luke bent everyone to his wishes.

They turned back to the manor, for suddenly Robin found that the elements were exhausting her, despite the look of tingling health they brought to her skin. At any other time she might have expected Luke to compliment her, but during the rest of that day it slowly dawned on her that Luke was taking her very much at her word. Apart from the mistletoe kisses, he acted the part of family friend, no more. She couldn't fault his impeccable manners, and he seemed attentive and relaxed. His apparent acceptance of her wishes left her piqued and suspicious. She didn't trust him. He wasn't the Luke she knew so well. She missed that other Luke. . . . She was definitely going soft in the head, Robin thought grimly.

The phone rang just after lunch on Boxing Day. When James answered it, he told Luke the call was for him. Luke was gone for ten minutes to answer it, and when he came back, there was something about his smile that made Robin's heart jolt a little.

"That was Carlotta," he told her, and she knew she'd been right to feel inexplicably chilled. "She's here in England to do some recordings. She arrived only an hour ago, phoned my house and got this number from my answering machine. She'll be staying in London for a week, and she's invited us both to a New Year's Eve party up there."

"Us? You mean me as well?" Robin echoed stupidly. Why on earth would Carlotta want her tagging along, unless it was to have her as a foil for her own dark Latin beauty!

"You as well, Robin," Luke said calmly. "Well, since I've enjoyed your father's hospitality here over Christmas, I thought taking you along to Carlotta's party would be a nice way of saying thank you. It'll be something to remember, I promise you. Carlotta never does anything by halves!"

I bet she doesn't, Robin thought angrily. She would refuse to go. She had no wish to see them together with her as the gooseberry. At James's query, Luke was explaining who Carlotta was, and her father evidently saw the New Year's Eve party as no more than a social occasion that sounded exciting.

"I'm sure you'll enjoy that, darling," he said. "It'll be a bit like old times, when you accompanied Elaine Fowler to some of her glittering parties, won't it? There may even be people there whom you know, if it's to do with the recording business. I'm glad you asked her, Luke. She needs something like this to put her back in top form again."

It was a conspiracy, Robin thought helplessly. She was being manipulated on all sides, and she wouldn't give in! But New Year's Eve had always seemed a particularly emotional time of the year to Robin, and not a time to spend alone. She met the briefest challenge in Luke's eyes. He expected her to refuse.

"I'd love to come, Luke," she heard herself say sweetly. "Thank you for asking me."

Chapter Twelve

She didn't have to extract a promise from Luke that they wouldn't stay in London overnight. He had a business meeting the next morning in a Bristol hotel with a Belgian hotelier who was only in town for a few days. As his secretary, Luke would need her there to take notes.

"I'm sorry I shall have to drag you away from the party soon after midnight, like Cinderella," Luke remarked as his car sped them along the motorway from Bristol to London.

"Please don't be," she said quickly. "I'm sure I'll have had enough by then, if the party is as glossy as some of those I attended with Mrs. Fowler!"

"Of course, you've been involved in this kind of thing before, haven't you, Robin?" He glanced at her in the darkened interior of the car. "Our Carlotta will be the star tonight, but you look very beautiful too. I'm proud to be your escort."

"Thank you."

Robin felt like weeping at these stilted platitudes. There seemed to be a barrier between them that grew higher every day. Since Carlotta's phone call, Luke had been more on edge than he had been since Robin had known him, and she wondered if he was regretting asking her to go with him.

All the closeness between them had vanished. It was as if he had never held her close to his heart so that their two hearts beat as one, as if his kisses had never taken her to heights of desire and awakened her to new and tumultuous sensations. As if he had never loved her. . . . She had to face the stark truth: Luke had never loved her. He had never pretended it was love he felt for her. And if she was to survive the evening, she had better play a part. She had no wish to be seen as the little lovesick secretary whom Luke had dragged along out of a sense of obligation. She would be as cool and sophisticated as she knew how.

Less than two hours later they were walking into the foyer of the huge London hotel, which glittered with lights and personalities from the TV and recording worlds. Carlotta greeted them at once, dazzlingly beautiful in red silk, jewels gleaming at her throat and in her hair. It was her show, all right, Robin realised.

She had a dark man in tow, Spanish like herself, whom she introduced as her record producer, Señor Juan Domingo. He was tall and elegant. When she suddenly became aware of what Carlotta was saying to Señor Domingo, Robin was struck by total disbelief.

"Juan, darling, this is Luke Burgess, whom you have heard me mention before and of whom you are most ridiculously jealous!" Carlotta oozed Latin charm at him, laughing as if the whole suggestion of her having any attachment to Luke were hilarious. "And this is Robin, his so-lovely English fiancée. Didn't I tell you that she has the most fabulous golden hair? Robin, darling, you look simply beautiful. Come and meet some people."

They were drawn into the melee before Robin could respond. It was only because she had met Carlotta before that she noted the slightest tremor in her voice as she made the outrageous introductions. And from the way Luke was gripping her arm as they moved into the main salon of the hotel, she knew exactly why he had brought her here—and why he had said nothing of his reasons before today. If he had done so, she would certainly never have come and been a party to this.

As Carlotta went off with her Juan to greet other newcomers, Robin saw her flash a look of gratitude towards Luke, but she had no chance to explode with fury for the moment. A couple of people whom she remembered from her days with Elaine Fowler suddenly recognised her and came rushing up to say hello.

"Robin, how marvellous you look. As soon as Carlotta mentioned your name, we thought it must be the same Robin Pollard we knew. And this is your fiancé, is it? Nice to meet you."

As someone more famous came into view they drifted off quickly, flitting like butterflies among the rich and the influential—but they didn't matter a damn right at that moment. What did matter was Luke's deception. Robin had expected to play a part that night, but not the part of his fiancée.

"How could you do this to me?" she grated at him, under cover of the noise and music blaring out from the salon. "It's just about the meanest trick you've played yet. If you think I'm going along with it—"

He leaned towards her, a smile on his face, looking for all the world as if he were an attentive lover, his arm around her waist, his mouth close to her cheek.

"You will because I say you will. It's only for this

one night, and I assure you it's not for any personal reasons. You've made it plain what you think of my advances, and I've no desire to jump into bed with a porcupine, whatever you think." He was deliberately crude, and when she gasped he pressed his lips to her mouth for a second, as lovingly as the part demanded. "Don't worry, once this party's over, we'll revert to our usual selves, dear Robin. This is for Carlotta, not for me. She's been crazy over Juan Domingo for months, and she wants to marry him. Being the hot-blooded Latin that he is, he somehow got the mistaken idea that Carlotta was smitten with me."

"I wonder why!" Robin snapped sarcastically.

"So when she phoned me at your father's house"—he went on as if she hadn't spoken, still playfully nuzzling her cheek as they mingled with the other guests—"she begged me to bring you along and let our so-called engagement be a decoy to cool Juan down a little. It's not meant to be anything more, if that's what's worrying you, Robin. I'm not insisting on any intimate scenes. Just look on it as part of the job. Many a boss has expected more from his secretary than one small harmless deception for one evening."

Robin looked at him angrily. His cool gaze gave nothing away. All this meant nothing to him, she thought sickly. He couldn't see what this pretend engagement would do to her, even for one evening. She thanked God that he couldn't guess.

"If I do this, will you release me from my obligation to stay on as your secretary until the complex is finished?" The words were out before she could stop them. Luke didn't answer for a minute. He must surely hear the pounding of her heart, even above the din, she thought. They were pressed so close that he must feel it.

"Providing you'll stay until I find a replacement," Luke said shortly.

"Done," she replied, feeling as if she were signing half of her life away. But she couldn't go on that way, seeing him every day, wanting him, loving him and knowing he wasn't for her. Even though, as it now appeared, Carlotta wasn't the woman in his life, there would always be another, and another. Hadn't all the signs pointed that way? She had Maureen's word on it and that of Mrs. Somerton, who knew him so well.

"Now that we've sealed the bargain, look the part, my darling," Luke said aggressively. "We don't want Juan to suspect that our relationship isn't perfect, do we? It would help if you pretended to have eyes for no one but me. Is it so impossible to pretend to be in love with me, just for a few hours?"

"I'll do my best," Robin murmured, raising luminous emerald eyes to meet his. He must never guess that the softness there was real, that as she melted against him with a little sigh when his arm tightened around her, Robin's heart was nearly breaking from the poignancy of all this. She loved him so much, and he was asking her to play the part of a woman in love! And so she would. They had made a bargain, and once this farce was over and Luke had kept his part of it and found a secretary to take her place, she could get out of his life for good. She could forget that Luke Burgess ever existed.

The dance music was romantic and dreamy, and Luke held her close. She wore a silvery dress and high-heeled shoes. Her only jewelry was her mother's emerald necklace and Luke's earrings. They moved together as one person. Robin closed her eyes as Luke's lips moved softly against her cheek, her hair, giving a superb performance of a man very much in love with the woman in his arms.

She tried to stay objective, to remember that this was solely for show—tried desperately not to let the ice around her heart melt as she was melting in his arms. Tomorrow this would be no more than a bittersweet memory to cherish for always, so for tonight why not forget all the hurt from the way Luke had got her there and let the fantasy continue? She was in his arms, where she most wanted to be, and all the tension between them was gone. He loved her, *he loved her,* and Robin loved him with a wild, sweet love that had no yesterday and no tomorrow. Only there, that night, the moment that Luke's deception had produced. *Enjoy it,* said her heart, *enjoy it while you can.*

"You're doing great," Luke whispered in her ear as the music finished. "I could almost believe you myself!"

She smiled up at him, hoping he wouldn't guess why the sparkle in her eyes was suddenly shimmer-bright. She hugged his arm, playing her part, playing it to heartbreaking perfection.

It was so easy to slip into the role of Luke's fiancée, so alarmingly sweet to believe that it wasn't pretence at all but the real thing. Especially at midnight, when by tradition all the lights went out for a moment and she was clasped in his arms and his mouth sought hers. Every sinew of his body possessed her for those timeless moments as he kissed her, and desire rippled through her like a flame, pulsating and uncontrollable. She gave an involuntary shudder at the exquisite sensations, and Luke released her at once, misconstruing her reaction.

"I apologise," he said in a ragged murmur. "Whether this engagement is true or false, I still find you a very desirable woman, Robin, and I'm afraid I got a little carried away."

Her eyes blurred, and she was thankful that the lights remained off for a few more seconds. If they hadn't, Luke would surely have seen the truth in her face. The cool mask was back in place by the time the room was ablaze with light once more.

"It's all right," she said huskily. "Luke, you did say we needn't stay long after midnight, didn't you? I'm beginning to feel tired, and it's a long drive home."

Normally she could have danced the night away and still have been ready for the office the next day. But this was no normal night, and her nerves had been strained to the limit. He nodded at once.

"We'll stay another ten minutes, then start making our good-byes if we can find Carlotta. I've had enough now too."

Robin swallowed. Enough of her, maybe. She couldn't blame him. A night such as this would probably end only one way for Luke Burgess, and with Robin it never did. Once, it had nearly happened. Funny now, to think it was Carlotta who had ended it. Carlotta, of whom Robin had been so jealous at the time and who hadn't been an important part of Luke's life after all. Funny . . . and yet not funny at all.

At last they were able to get away, and from the beaming smiles on Carlotta's and Juan's faces, Robin and Luke had made a good job of their so-called engagement. Presumably, in time, when Carlotta had a gold wedding ring on her finger, she might tell her husband casually that her two English friends had called the whole thing off. And he might just say how sad, when they had looked so right for each other.

Robin stopped tormenting herself, making her mind a blank as they drove back along the motorway, truthfully very tired now. Luke told her to sleep if she wanted to, and though she fought against it, sleep overcame her. She awoke with some embarrassment to find her head leaning against Luke's shoulder as he stopped the car at her flat.

"Are you all right?" His voice was distant, his question no more than a polite enquiry. They might never again be as close as they had been all that evening.

"I'm fine," she lied. "What time in the morning, Luke?"

"I'll be here for you at ten-thirty. It's not an early session. Sleep well, and thank you for tonight, Robin."

She nearly said it was her pleasure, but the words stuck in her throat. They would sound either like an invitation or appallingly sarcastic, and she didn't want either meaning taken at that moment. She just wanted to sleep, to blot out the entire evening from her mind, the pleasure and the pain.

"Good night," she said, closing the car door and trying not to run into the building as the need to be alone overwhelmed her. She heard Luke's car as he drove around the green to his own house. It might have been an ocean that separated them. Cinderella had been to the ball, but for her the good times were over. There was no Prince Charming.

Robin's pride kept her from asking Luke if he wanted her to write the ad for a new secretary, though if he hadn't done it by the end of the week, she intended to draft it and leave it on his desk for his approval. After a meeting with a Belgian client, he had gone off to look over a possible site for a luxury hotel at Ostend. He wouldn't be back until the weekend. It gave her a breathing space, but she knew then that she wouldn't change her mind. It was impossible to continue working with him.

A phone call around four A.M. on Friday morning sent all thoughts of Luke out of her mind. She struggled awake at the insistent ringing, her heart thumping at once. Nobody called at that hour unless it was bad news.

"Is that you, Robin?" Mrs. Drew's voice said anxiously.

"Yes. What's happened? Is it Dad?" It had to be, of course.

"Now, don't get panicky, dear. He didn't want me to ring you until later, but I thought you'd want to know at once. He's in the hospital in Penzance."

"Hospital!" Robin's heart hammered so fast that she could hardly breathe. Memories of the traumatic morning she had found her employer dead seemed to leap into her mind, drying her mouth.

"He was taken ill last evening, dear, but he just kept joking that it was my cooking. Then some time after he'd gone to bed I heard him shouting out. He was in such pain I sent for the doctor, and I'm afraid it was a burst appendix. They're operating on him right now. I'm sorry to ring you with such news, my love, and you must forgive me for going all watery on you, but I've been with you both for such a long time. . . ."

The sound of sniffling at the other end of the line jolted Robin out of her initial panic. She made herself think practically.

"I'll get the first train out of here this morning, Mrs. Drew, and go straight to the hospital. Will you phone them to tell Dad I'm on my way, so that he knows it as soon as he comes around?"

"I will, Robin. And I'll have a hot meal prepared for you this evening. You'll be staying over the weekend, I presume?" Robin could hear the relief in Mrs. Drew's voice.

"Yes, of course." Longer than that, Robin thought, longer than that. "I'll see you later, Mrs. Drew."

Her hands were still shaking when she had hung up

the phone. She had a purpose now: Luke Burgess didn't need her, but her father did. Perhaps Luke would see that as letting him down, but she had his word that he would look for a new secretary, and her father's illness merely necessitated her leaving earlier than she had planned. She wouldn't think of Luke now.

She would have to come back to Bristol to collect everything she had brought and all that she had acquired since arriving there—the things that had turned the flat into a home. But that could wait. Right now, she had to find out train times and order a taxi to get her to the station. She flipped through the local directory and began dialling the numbers.

By the time the rest of the city was waking up, Robin was sitting on the early train, travelling west, a hastily packed suitcase on the rack. She shivered in the cold wintery morning, snuggling down into the fur collar of her coat, hardly noticing the bleak, cheerless countryside speeding past the window.

It had been too early to phone anyone at the office, but Robin knew that Luke's answering machine at the office would be operating, so she had left a brief message saying where she had gone and why and that she would be in touch once she had seen her father. Naturally, Luke would want to know how James was faring. They were bound together by the holiday complex. *Business partners . . . business partners . . .* the words seemed to drum through her head to the rhythm of the train, cold and unemotional. It was the way she must try to think of Luke Burgess from then on.

Robin moved restlessly, seeing her own darkened reflection in the window of the train. Her hair was more dishevelled than usual. She pushed her fingers through it, and the memory of Luke's hands parting the fine golden strands so sensuously was instantly, poignantly, in her mind. She seemed to see him everywhere, to hear his voice, to feel his touch, and her eyes were damp as she closed them, knowing that what she asked of herself was nearly impossible.

The only way she could cope was to get out of his life, and that was what she intended to do. Since it was certain he would be visiting Pollard Manor from time to time in connection with the complex, Robin herself must get a job well away from there. Once she was sure her father was well again, she would go to London and become one of the anonymous thousands. What James had said was true, Robin thought suddenly: She had changed. Once the thought of living and working in the city would have appalled her. Now, because of Luke, she was fleeing from her very roots, and it was the city that was her haven. It was one more thing to hold against him.

Robin went straight to the hospital from the Penzance station. She hated those places, with their antiseptic smells and closed-in atmospheres. But then, she was grateful for all their skills when she was told that James had had a completely successful operation and had just gone back to the ward.

"He's still very woozy after the anesthetic," the Sister told her. "But since you've come so far, you can see him for a few minutes, my dear. By visiting time tonight he'll be a new man."

It was the Sister who took her along to the ward, where the screens were still around the bed nearest the door. Behind them James was paler than usual and unfamiliarly inactive, but his eyes widened with gladness as he saw Robin approach the bed and lean over quickly to kiss his dry lips.

"How did you get here so fast?" he said in a thready voice. "I told Mrs. Drew not to worry you."

"Don't be silly, Dad." Robin's eyes filled with

tears. "Of course she had to tell me. I'd have been furious if she hadn't!"

She tried to sound indignant to cover her relief at seeing him. He gave a weak laugh and then winced.

"I musn't do that," he muttered. "I feel like dancing to see you, darling, but it'll be a while before I do that again."

"And I'm staying here until you do," she said firmly.

"Staying?" James echoed. "What about Luke and your job?"

"He can do without me," she said, her heart twisting at the truth of the statement.

"But not for long, Robin. You can't leave him in the lurch just because of me. I shall soon be over this, and there's no reason for you to stay."

Robin was aware that her father was getting agitated, and the Sister was hovering. She spoke quickly.

"Of course not for long, Dad. Don't worry. Luke will understand. I'll be talking to him tonight when he gets back from Ostend. If he'd been around, I know he'd have insisted on driving me down here himself. We both care about you, you know. I'm going home for a welcome hot meal, now that I've seen that you're all right. I'll be back tonight."

She bent and kissed him again, fighting back the tears. What she had said was the truth. Luke did care about her father's welfare, and not just for commercial reasons. She gave him that much credit. The two of them had always hit it off admirably, and she didn't want to worry her father with the news that she was no longer officially in Luke's employ.

Once she had left the hospital and begun an extravagant taxi ride all the way to Pollard Manor, Robin leaned back in the smoothly purring car, mentally exhausted but certain of one thing: James must be kept in ignorance of her decision as long as possible.

And that meant Mrs. Drew as well. Both of them must believe she was there only until James was home again and well on the way back to health.

By the time she had listened to Mrs. Drew's tearful account of the frantic time during the night, eaten the first food since a scrappy piece of toast that morning and been back to the hospital, where James was sitting up and looking considerably better, Robin felt as if the slightest breeze would blow her away. And she still had to phone Luke. She couldn't put it off any longer. He'd be back by that time, and he'd have got the messages from his answering machine. Even as she hedged about, the phone rang, and she knew before she picked it up that it would be Luke.

"How is he?" he said at once, with no preamble.

"Much brighter this evening," Robin stammered. His voice sounded so near, almost as if she could reach out her hand and touch him. She pictured him at home, leaning against the wall of the lounge the way he did, his fingers curled around the receiver. She was becoming light-headed.

"Luke, I'm—I'm sorry, but I had to come as soon as Mrs. Drew phoned me."

"Of course you did. And you'll stay awhile, naturally."

She took a deep breath. "I'm staying, Luke. For good. I'll have to come back sometime for the rest of my things, but you can ask Mrs. Somerton to pack them up for me if you need the flat for someone else. Otherwise, as soon as Dad's home and better, I'll drive up and collect everything myself."

There was a pause at the other end.

"I see. You've made up your mind, then." There was no anger or even surprise in his voice, Robin thought dully. It was as if he expected it and he didn't care.

"We did discuss it, if you remember. Now that this

has happened, it seems the best way," she said jerkily, glad he couldn't see that her eyes were filled with tears.

"Just as you wish. Give your father my very best wishes. I would call and see him if I were coming down to the site in the near future, but that doesn't seem likely. There are some problems with the Belgian deal, and I have to go back there next week. I can't expect you to be interested in such details now, of course. I'll phone Maggie and see if she'll come back on a temporary basis, though I still consider you in my employ for the time being. I haven't fired you, and I don't recall seeing your notice in writing. Let's just call this a temporary break in our arrangement, shall we?"

"Luke, I—I can't—"

"Call me anytime if you need me." The phone went dead.

Chapter Thirteen

Robin wasn't aware that she stood there with tears streaming down her face, her whole body shaking, until she felt Mrs. Drew take the phone from her hand and replace it. She felt the motherly arms go round her trembling shoulders, and a paper tissue was pushed into her hand.

"There, my love, it's been a trying time for you, but your father's a strong man and it'll take more than an old burst appendix to finish him off! He'll be out of there in double-quick time, you'll see. And whatever differences you and that young man of yours have had, it's my advice to you to go back to Bristol and sort them out face to face. It's always the best way. Now, I'm going to make us both a nice hot cup of tea—unless you'd rather have a stiff brandy."

"No, thank you, Mrs. Drew." Robin smiled weakly at the way she was being taken over. She was always the strong one, but right now it felt so good to let Mrs. Drew boss her about. It was obvious she had overheard Robin's side of the phone conversation and got it all wrong about her and Luke! She probably saw it as a lovers' tiff, but Robin knew it was better not to try to explain or she'd be blurting out everything to Mrs. Drew's sympathetic ear, and she had no intention of doing so. She wiped her eyes and blew her nose.

"Tea will be lovely," she said thinly. "And if you've got any of your fruitcake about, I think I could manage a piece of that as well."

"That's right. There's no man on earth worth losing your appetite for," Mrs. Drew said soothingly.

Robin could have told her that it wasn't lack of food that was causing the emptiness inside her, but being practical as well as emotional, she knew she had better start acting as normally as possible at Pollard Manor, because everything would be reported back to her father. She didn't want him worrying on her account. He had to concentrate on getting well.

By the end of a week the old Cornish magic had begun to weave its spell. There were still times when Robin awoke in the night from a dream of Luke that was so vivid, so real, that she almost reached out her hand to touch him, to welcome his kiss. She couldn't forget. It was impossible to think that she ever would, but she was prepared to let time and distance lessen the pain a little.

And James would be discharged from the hospital once his stitches were removed. There had been no complications, and his strong constitution and determination of will had seen him through very quickly. Luke had phoned several more times to enquire after him, always in the same stilted manner, with no more personal comments. It was just as if he had shut her out of his life as much as was possible. Numbly, Robin told herself it was what she wanted.

If she had fooled Luke, it was harder to fool her

father. He had known her too long and was able to read the cause for her shadowed eyes quite correctly. He knew her volatile temper, too, and wisely said nothing for the time being, though he was filled with impatience at the shortsightedness of the two people for whom he cared.

"You don't have to stay indefinitely, Robin," James said mildly as they sat drinking coffee one morning. January had turned unexpectedly mild, and they sat in the glass conservatory, sheltered from the sea breezes and warmed by the thin rays of sunlight. They lit Robin's hair with golden glints, and the anxiety of past weeks had made her cheeks finely drawn, giving her an ethereal look.

"I won't," she replied, forcing lightness into her voice. "Don't worry, I'm only staying until I can trust you not to go galloping off to inspect the building site; then I'm off."

He recognised her teasing and the fact that mention of Luke's complex had made her lips tremble. It would take very little to push her over the edge, James realised worriedly. And it was all so ridiculous when she and Luke were made for each other. Any fool could see that, even if Robin and Luke couldn't.

He allowed her to mope about the place for one more week. She had driven into Helston one morning to return James's library books. James called out to her the minute she got back. He was looking vastly better by then, Robin thought thankfully, and was practically his old self.

"Luke phoned," James said at once, causing her heart to leap, miss a beat and then thud rapidly.

"Really?" She tried to be indifferent. "I hope you told him that you're like a bear with a sore head, wanting to do everything at once, now you're on the mend."

"He's ill, Robin. I could hardly make out his voice,

it was so thick and muffled. He needs you back urgently. Maggie someone-or-other has had to cry off taking over for you, and there're some urgent papers that need attention, and Luke won't trust them to the office junior."

Robin heard only the first two words. All the rest was irrelevant.

"Luke's ill?" she whispered. "What's wrong with him?"

"He didn't say, but he's at home, and if you go straight there, he'll tell you what needs to be done," James said briskly. He glanced at his watch. "You can be there soon after lunchtime if you hurry, so what are you waiting for? I'd grab a bite to eat at a motorway service station if I were you."

"Will you be all right, Dad?"

"Good Lord, woman, I'm not made of glass! Get your priorities right and go where you're most needed! Phone me tonight to let me know how things are."

Robin bent and kissed him, the only thought in her mind that Luke needed her. It didn't matter why. Nor did she bother to analyse why she was prepared to drive back to Bristol, when normally she hated driving long distances. Luke was ill and he needed her, and she must go. For once she wasn't looking for reasons. She was letting her heart rule her head.

She stopped once, to stretch her legs and get something to eat as James had suggested. She'd be no good to Luke if she arrived feeling faint from hunger. She still managed to arrive at Luke's house a little after two in the afternoon, thanking her lucky stars that there had been no snow yet that winter, or she'd never have made it.

The house looked welcoming. Luke's house, Robin thought, with a little catch of emotion as she pulled into the driveway. Bristol was colder than Cornwall, but oddly it still felt like coming home. It was a dangerously poignant thought, and one that she mustn't dwell upon.

Knowing the layout of the house and thinking that Luke might be sleeping, Robin quietly opened the kitchen door and let herself in, anticipating Mrs. Somerton's ready smile. The room was empty, as tidy as ever. Robin went through to the lounge, leaving her thick coat on the hall coatrack.

Then she stopped dead, standing very still at the sight that met her eyes. In the fireplace a roaring log fire sent flames leaping up the chimney, warm and welcoming. On the sideboard was a beautiful winter flower arrangement of reds and greens, adding a glow to the room. On a small side table a decanter of sherry gleamed like liquid gold in the firelight as Luke began to fill two glasses from it.

A strong, virile, ruggedly handsome and healthy Luke turned to hand one of the glasses to her, a wary smile curving his lips as he awaited her reaction. In an instant Robin registered it all.

She finally found her voice. She was burning with anger, her face heated, her expressive eyes flashing emerald fire. Any other man but Luke would have backed off at such a look, but Luke just kept coming forward, like a panther stalking its prey. She stepped back a pace, her hands clenched so tightly that her nails bit into her palms.

"You—you swine!" Robin ground out. "You unspeakable liar! You aren't ill at all, are you? It was all one of your clever schemes to get me back here, wasn't it? And you had the nerve to involve my father in it too."

Hot tears threatened to fill her eyes, and she blinked them back furiously. She had cried in front of Luke Burgess for the last time.

"How could you be so insensitive?" she raged on. "I thought you always called Dad your business partner. Is this the way you treat your partners? By deceiving them to get what you want?"

Luke had put the sherry glasses down. He came close to her so swiftly, there was no chance for her to avoid his steellike hold on her arms. She glared up at him, seeing the muscles at the sides of his strong mouth working slightly. He wasn't used to being thwarted, Robin thought scornfully, holding on to every bit of fury she could, because if she let her guard drop just once, she was perfectly capable of melting into his arms, and she knew it.

"Your father said you were always prone to tantrums," Luke snapped back at her, making her gasp with outrage. "When he phoned me this morning and we cooked up this little plan, he said that if you still acted stubbornly, I had his permission to put you over my knee and smack some sense into you."

Robin's mouth opened wide. Just what was going on?

"Dad phoned you?" she asked suspiciously. "That's not the way I heard it. He said you phoned him to say that you were ill, and your voice was—"

"Thick and muffled." He used James's exact phrase. "That's the way he said it, wasn't it? We had to make it convincing. He doesn't need you to nursemaid him any longer, Robin, and we both decided that my needs were greater than his."

"Your needs!" She bristled again at that. "Everybody knows what your needs are, don't they? Carlotta or any one of a score of girls could supply those."

"Carlotta's marrying Juan Domingo at the end of the month," he told her, still with the steely edge to his voice that told her he wasn't as much in control as he'd like her to think. She knew him too well not to be able to recognise every nuance in his voice by then. "And why you have this ridiculous idea that I have scores of women falling at my feet, I can't imagine."

"I don't want to talk about your women," Robin snapped.

He suddenly shook her violently. Robin cried out, shocked at this new side of him.

"There's only one woman I care about, and that's the woman in my arms, the most stubborn woman it's been my misfortune to meet."

"Then the sooner we sever all connections with each other, the better," Robin said icily. With an effort she pulled away from him, fighting off the dull inevitability of what she was saying. "Since I'm here, I'll go across to the flat and pick up the rest of my things. You did me a favour after all, bringing me here. Once I've packed up everything in my car, I need never come back here again."

She gave an involuntary swallow and knew that he saw it. He knew her weakness. She made herself look away from that searching, glowering gaze, afraid that he would read the naked truth in her eyes. The nearness of him, her need for him, was driving her mad. She had to get away from him before she betrayed the yearning and the love she felt.

"May I remind you that you came here today to work," he said coldly. "There's one last item I want you to do for me. After that, go if you must. I won't detain you. I don't force my women to stay."

The little twist to his mouth as he repeated something he'd said once before was almost real enough to give the lie to Luke's being a womaniser. But Robin told herself ruthlessly that she believed that only because she wanted to.

"What is it you want?" she said, pointedly ignoring all the rest.

Luke moved to a drawer in the sideboard, almost throwing a notebook and pencil at her.

"Take my dictation." His voice was terse, and she

realised he was as tense as she was. She sat down heavily in an armchair, suddenly feeling as if every nerve and bone in her body was aching from this meeting. The sooner it was over, the better. Then she would get out of his life forever.

Robin leaned over the pad, flipping it open to a blank page. Her fine hair hung around her face, hiding her expression from Luke's intense eyes, the firelight turning it to gold. She waited as he stood with his back to the fire, facing her, darkly etched against the leaping flames behind him, like some demonic figure.

He began speaking evenly, the rich timbre of his voice filling the room as her fingers flew across the page.

"This is to terminate our business arrangement," Luke said at his dictating speed, deliberate and thoughtful. "And to inform you that your services are no longer required."

Robin looked up, renewed colour sweeping into her cheeks.

"How can you be so cruel as to humiliate me like this?"

"I haven't said this notice is for you yet," he retorted.

She knew for certain that it was. And he was doing it in order to turn the knife that little bit more. Robin was the one woman who hadn't fallen completely for his charm, and this was his way of paying her back. Oh, if only he knew . . . if only he knew. . . .

"Will you continue, please? You're still working for me for the moment." As she nodded, biting her lips, Luke went on. His next words made it obvious that she was right. This letter was intended for her.

"As you know, I have a business partnership with your father. In due time his interest in the complex will become yours, and you and I will be partners. That arrangement would seem to be unacceptable to us both."

Robin could hardly see the page now, but she was determined to carry on. Whether she would be able to decipher her shorthand was uncertain, but his words were indelibly written on her heart.

"So, since I find it unthinkable to contemplate spending the rest of my life without you, Miss Pollard, I propose offering you another partnership, one that would take place as quickly as possible."

Robin's hands froze, no longer scribbling. Had she really heard him right? Her head jerked up to meet his steady gaze. Her heart beat so fast, so fast. Almost incredulously she saw Luke's steely controlled expression change. For one breathless moment he looked oddly vulnerable, his sensual mouth curving at one side as he brushed one hand through his dark hair in a gesture of frustration. Thickly he uttered a small oath.

"How much plainer do I have to make it, Robin? These few weeks without you have been sheer hell. I'm no good with words, and I've resisted telling any woman that I loved her until I found the one I wanted to be my wife and share the rest of my life. I waited so long that it was more difficult to finally say it than I ever imagined it would be. But you must know that I love you! You must have known it in Ibiza. Didn't you *know* that was what I was saying with everything but words!"

He didn't say any more, because Robin had jumped up with a little cry of pure joy. Luke held open his arms and she went straight into them. For someone who didn't have the words, he had managed to get his meaning across very clearly, she thought ecstatically. Then all thoughts and words were superfluous as his mouth met hers in a sweet, savage kiss that seemed as if it would never end. And all the pent-up emotions and frustrations between them dissolved like a Cornish mist.

"I'm not dreaming all this, am I?" Robin murmured when the kiss finally ended and she was still held close to his heart, which was beating as heavily as her own.

"If you are, then I'm dreaming, too, and let's hope we'll never wake up." Luke's voice was still husky, and she felt the sweet familiar caress of his hands on her arms, her shoulders, her hair. She felt his passion in every masculine throb of his body, in every whisper-soft touch of his lips against her cheek and throat.

"I can't quite believe this." Robin's voice was becoming throaty, too, as her own body responded with intensely pleasurable sensations to the unspoken demands of his. "Did I really hear you say you loved me, Luke?"

"You did, woman, and you'd better get used to hearing it, now that I've discovered it isn't so hard to say. I love you, Robin, I love you. It's something I haven't heard from you yet, though."

He drew her down with him onto the thick carpet. Bathed in firelight, she looked into the dear face of her beloved and caught her breath.

"Do I need to tell you?"

"It seems you do, my darling," Luke said, with a brief return to his old aggressive masculinity. "Men have the same need as women to be told the obvious at certain times in their lives. We have feelings, too, you know. So put me out of my misery and tell me you love me and you're going to marry me!"

Robin couldn't resist laughing a little at that, sheer happiness dancing in her eyes as the music of his words flowed over her.

"Yes, sir," she mocked him. "I know you don't like your secretary to embellish your words, but this time

I'll just add to it, if you don't mind. I love you, Luke. I love you so much it nearly cut me to shreds on New Year's Eve when you made me act the part of your fiancée for Carlotta's sake. For a little while it all seemed so real."

"And now it's going to be real," Luke said fiercely. He stroked the soft, silky hair spread out against the carpet. He drew in his breath at the love he saw in her glowing eyes, then looked a little shamefaced.

"It was a rotten thing to put you through, my dearest, and I know it. But Carlotta was desperate to make Juan believe there was nothing between her and me. There never was—not in the way you thought. It wasn't until we were coming back to Bristol that night that I guessed what an ordeal it must have been for you. Then, of course, you wanted to be released from our arrangement at the office, and I thought you had turned against me for good."

"Are you telling me you loved me even then?" Robin whispered. She felt his fingers on her cheek, trailing downwards to the neckline of her blouse, to the pulsing beat of her heart.

"I've loved you from the day I first saw you in your Cornish cove, protesting so eloquently that I was invading your space. I didn't think of it as love then, of course. You were more of an irritation under my skin, although a very beautiful one! It was only later, when you had infiltrated my heart so that I couldn't even sleep at nights for wanting you, that I knew it was love. But you were always so suspicious of me and my motives. I knew that if I told you I loved you, you wouldn't believe me." He shrugged. "It seemed the only way I could get through to you was to keep up the brash image you'd given me and hope you might decide to try and reform me!"

"Oh, Luke," Robin breathed softly. "All this precious time we've wasted."

She felt him unfasten the buttons of her blouse, and his hand moved inside to caress her breast. Seconds later, as his mouth followed where his fingers had led, a tingling warmth filled Robin's veins as she closed her eyes, totally cocooned in Luke's love.

"Don't let's waste any more time," he said against the softness of her flesh. "We have the house to ourselves for the day, Robin. And as soon as we can get a certain special license, we'll have the rest of our lives together."

"Starting now," she whispered, knowing that no time could be more right for them than there and then. In the firelight the union of hearts and minds and bodies made a vow as binding as any marriage troth.

Still feeling as if it were all part of a dream from which she must surely awaken soon, Robin shed her clothes in trembling haste, following Luke's lead. And when at last he lay with her, his lean, hard body fitting against hers so perfectly as she matched his every movement, Robin knew at last the meaning of fulfillment between a man and a woman.

Nothing less than love could extract the ultimate explosive pleasure Luke gave her. Nothing less than love could make his rich male voice thicken with emotion as he told her that that was only the beginning of their lives—that everything until then had been leading up to that.

Luke told her he loved her over and over again, as if the words, once unleashed from him, were as natural as breathing. Robin felt completely secure in Luke's love, giving him back touch for touch, kiss for kiss, learning the needs of a man with exquisite pleasure, loving the teacher too much to feel any embarrassment.

That day Luke had made her feel a woman for the first time in her life. As she lay drowsily in his arms, the first passion spent, she stroked the skin of his shoulder, pressing her lips to the muscle.

A small bubbling laugh rose to her throat as she told him he'd have to start looking for a new secretary after all.

"That's a minor problem." Luke ran his hands down the curving line of her body, as if to memorise its perfection forever. "I can always get a new secretary. I'm far more interested in signing you up for the one job for which you'll be the only applicant. How do you feel about being my partner for life, my lovely Robin? My partner in love."

"Don't you know how I feel?" she answered huskily. "I thought that was perfectly obvious."

She didn't require an answer, and neither did she mind that Luke seemed to have run out of words for the time being. Instead he gathered her up in his arms again. She tasted the sweetness of his mouth on hers, and she gave a small breathless sigh of pleasure as Luke began making love to her all over again.

IT'S YOUR OWN SPECIAL TIME

Contemporary romances for today's women.
Each month, six very special love stories will be yours
from SILHOUETTE.

$1.75 each

- ☐ 100 Stanford
- ☐ 101 Hardy
- ☐ 102 Hastings
- ☐ 103 Cork
- ☐ 104 Vitek
- ☐ 105 Eden
- ☐ 106 Dailey
- ☐ 107 Bright
- ☐ 108 Hampson
- ☐ 109 Vernon
- ☐ 110 Trent
- ☐ 111 South
- ☐ 112 Stanford
- ☐ 113 Browning
- ☐ 114 Michaels
- ☐ 115 John
- ☐ 116 Lindley
- ☐ 117 Scott
- ☐ 118 Dailey
- ☐ 119 Hampson
- ☐ 120 Carroll
- ☐ 121 Langan
- ☐ 122 Scofield
- ☐ 123 Sinclair
- ☐ 124 Beckman
- ☐ 125 Bright
- ☐ 126 St. George
- ☐ 127 Roberts
- ☐ 128 Hampson
- ☐ 129 Converse
- ☐ 130 Hardy
- ☐ 131 Stanford
- ☐ 132 Wisdom
- ☐ 133 Rowe
- ☐ 134 Charles
- ☐ 135 Logan
- ☐ 136 Hampson
- ☐ 137 Hunter
- ☐ 138 Wilson
- ☐ 139 Vitek
- ☐ 140 Erskine
- ☐ 142 Browning
- ☐ 143 Roberts
- ☐ 144 Goforth
- ☐ 145 Hope
- ☐ 146 Michaels
- ☐ 147 Hampson
- ☐ 148 Cork
- ☐ 149 Saunders
- ☐ 150 Major
- ☐ 151 Hampson
- ☐ 152 Halston
- ☐ 153 Dailey
- ☐ 154 Beckman
- ☐ 155 Hampson
- ☐ 156 Sawyer
- ☐ 157 Vitek
- ☐ 158 Reynolds
- ☐ 159 Tracy
- ☐ 160 Hampson
- ☐ 161 Trent
- ☐ 162 Ashby
- ☐ 163 Roberts
- ☐ 164 Browning
- ☐ 165 Young
- ☐ 166 Wisdom
- ☐ 167 Hunter
- ☐ 168 Carr
- ☐ 169 Scott
- ☐ 170 Ripy
- ☐ 171 Hill
- ☐ 172 Browning
- ☐ 173 Camp
- ☐ 174 Sinclair
- ☐ 175 Jarrett
- ☐ 176 Vitek
- ☐ 177 Dailey
- ☐ 178 Hampson
- ☐ 179 Beckman
- ☐ 180 Roberts
- ☐ 181 Terrill
- ☐ 182 Clay
- ☐ 183 Stanley
- ☐ 184 Hardy
- ☐ 185 Hampson
- ☐ 186 Howard
- ☐ 187 Scott
- ☐ 188 Cork
- ☐ 189 Stephens
- ☐ 190 Hampson
- ☐ 191 Browning
- ☐ 192 John
- ☐ 193 Trent
- ☐ 194 Barry
- ☐ 195 Dailey
- ☐ 196 Hampson
- ☐ 197 Summers
- ☐ 198 Hunter
- ☐ 199 Roberts
- ☐ 200 Lloyd
- ☐ 201 Starr
- ☐ 202 Hampson
- ☐ 203 Browning
- ☐ 204 Carroll
- ☐ 205 Maxam
- ☐ 206 Manning
- ☐ 207 Windham

$1.95 each

- ☐ 208 Halston
- ☐ 209 LaDame
- ☐ 210 Eden
- ☐ 211 Walters
- ☐ 212 Young
- ☐ 213 Dailey
- ☐ 214 Hampson
- ☐ 215 Roberts
- ☐ 216 Saunders
- ☐ 217 Vitek
- ☐ 218 Hunter
- ☐ 219 Cork
- ☐ 220 Hampson
- ☐ 221 Browning
- ☐ 222 Carroll
- ☐ 223 Summers

Coming Next Month

Journey To Quiet Waters by Dixie Browning

Ivy had regretted the sale of her family estate. And now Hunter Smith, the new owner, arrogantly demanded the use of the house *and* her services—and soon captured her heart as well.

Behind Closed Doors by Diana Morgan

Troubleshooter Spencer McIntyre had been called in to untangle the mess Emily Moreau had playfully programmed into the company computer. Now the computer seemed determined to get the battling couple together.

Beloved Pirate by Ann Cockcroft

Laura knew that famous author Jared Tanner had earned his reputation as an unscrupulous lover. But on the romantic Spanish island of Mallorca, common sense—and her fiance back home—seemed very far away.

That Tender Feeling by Dorothy Vernon

Ros Seymour was a top-notch chef but somehow she couldn't seem to do anything right when devastating Cliff Heath was around. It seemed she'd need more than her culinary skills to convince him they were meant to be together.

South Of The Sun by Laurie Paige

It was a physical challenge to be the only woman on an expedition to the desolate wilderness of the South Pole, but Jordie soon found a greater challenge in resisting the impossibly attractive scientist Jarl Ericson.

A Separate Happiness by Brittany Young

Brianna knew that Caesare De Alvarado was playing a dangerous and deadly game to help his people. Their love could be fatal, but try as she might, Brianna couldn't stay away.